I Have a Story

by

Colleen L. Donnelly

I Have a Story

Cover Art by *Teddi Black*

The Wild Rose Press, Inc.
PO Box 708
Adams Basin, NY 14410-0708
Visit us at www.thewildrosepress.com

Publishing History
First Edition, 2025
Trade Paperback ISBN 978-1-5092-6132-1
Digital ISBN 978-1-5092-6133-8

Published in the United States of America

Dedication

I owe the inspiration to write this book to my editor, Nan Swanson. The award for patience goes to my husband who barely saw me once the writing began.

Chapter 1

Seth Linden belonged to the world of publishing. I did as well, and had for several years, as his top crime-writing novelist. My sales had soared as America anticipated what appeared to be a second world war brewing overseas; news which failed to erase Seth's apprehensive scowl as he greeted me. The US rightly reeled between terror and thrill at entering such a major battle, but he reeled at how it or any situation would affect his pocketbook. Seth preferred control internationally and personally and therefore wasn't going to respond well to the bomb I had come to his office to drop on him today.

"Well, Jim, I presume you are here to announce your next story idea now that the corrupt law enforcement series is finished." Seth's wary expression revealed he didn't presume any such thing. Curly headed, barely over thirty but carrying a slight paunch, he peered across his desk at me through eyeglasses too small for his face. Ours was a writer-vs-editor love-hate relationship we both accepted, and which had worked well for us ever since I began writing for him. I didn't expect that to hold true for us today.

His uneasiness intensified as I considered the best response. I was the one who had a way with words. Carelessness on my part, and Seth might not survive my announcement that I intended to take a break from crime writing to seek out a different type of story. My grandfather's story. The only one he never told me. And no matter how unbelievable I suspected it might turn out to be, I would pursue it because he wanted me to.

Seth narrowed one eye. "You didn't come here for plot chit-chat, did you? I can see it on your face. If you are toying with the idea of enlisting ahead of the draft if America joins this war, let me remind you of what I say every time—You have far more impact with your typewriter here in the States than you would by carrying a rifle overseas in a face-off with Hitler. Trust me. I wouldn't lie to you."

Seth would lie. He often did. He said whatever it took to keep me writing highly popular crime novels for his publishing house and war-related articles for the *Times*, New York's largest newspaper, the latter to convince the government of my usefulness close to home instead of in the army.

In an office that reeked of paper and ink, I settled in for his lengthy reminder that he had turned my stories into America's distraction from the atrocities in Europe, my face into one people trusted, and my words about other twenty-six-year-old men, or even younger ones, into reasons for the US to rally behind its heroes.

I scratched an imaginary itch through the knee of what I termed fake-tweed slacks, America's clothing industry rightly shifting its resources to what its soldiers would need if we joined the war. I uncrossed my legs and straightened in the uncomfortable wooden chair. For all Seth's assurance of my value to the world, he missed the one thing I also had missed for years: my grandfather's definition of a true hero…

Heroes aren't heroes because they are clever or

brave, but because they love someone or something deeply.

I knew by heart every wise word my grandfather had ever spoken, but not one had I taken to heart. Maybe it was his end-of-life frailty that hit me square in the face the other day, or maybe it was my age. But for the first time, I paid attention to what Grandpa, my hero as a man and as a storyteller, had said—it's what motivates a man that matters. What motivated him shone deep in his gaze, while what motivated Seth and me was the success my storytelling skills brought our way.

Seth rambled on, deep into his too-familiar monologue about all the good he and I had done, while I kicked myself for time lost with my grandfather. For ignoring what he had inserted into every one of his tales with the hope I would someday understand it—love, or anything to do with the heart. I had inherited his ability to tell a story but not his essence. He claimed it was in me; I just hadn't found it yet. In truth, I spent little time looking for something that had no place in my books.

Look for the relationship when you write, son. There always is one, whether it is between a man and a woman, a boy and his dog, a sailor and his ship, or a country and its enemy. The most daring conquests involve the heart. There is no battle, no story, until there is heart.

Heart. Not a word found in Seth's vocabulary or my stories. I twisted in my seat. Grandpa never said outright that my books lacked heart. Rather, he praised every single one for its well-constructed plot. He was a truly good man. When had he begun to look so frail, so sallow...

"Are you listening to me?" Seth frowned across mountains of contracts and manuscripts that cluttered his desktop. "If you are still fantasizing about enlisting, let me remind you that you are too thin to wield a gun. America needs Jim Turner here, not over there."

I bit back a rebuttal of Seth's slight against the lanky build I had also inherited from my grandfather, both of us tall and lean with straight hair, mine brown, his face handsome, mine what Seth called a pensive writer's look that people adored. At least the current style of baggy trousers and blousy shirts cinched tight by a belt looked far better on us than it did on him.

"I heard you," I semi-lied to Seth's pointed expression. At least I had heard it before. "I will enlist at some point, so brace yourself, but not yet. I have something else to do first."

"Whatever it is, I won't like it. I can tell." Seth tilted back in his office chair, which let out its usual squeal, causing a fantasy other than the one he worried about to pop into my head—Seth tipping a tad too far and somersaulting backward through his office's plate-glass window. We were two stories up. He might survive. But someone in New York City's throng down below might not.

"It has to do with my grandfather…" And what he hadn't said all these years, as well as the way he looked at me the last time we spoke.

"Oh no, not this again. I like him, I adore him, in fact, but let's face it. If you listen to Grandpa Turner too much, you will be writing dime romance novels instead of your hard-hitting crime stories that sell like hotcakes."

A fist formed in my gut. I might be thin, but I could land a punch with words my opponent would be slow to get up from, and Seth deserved it. "Did I tell you my idea for a new captivating storyline?"

"That's more like it." Seth righted himself and his chair. "Tell me about that instead."

"An editor's body washes up on the bank of the Hudson River."

Seth stared across his desk at me. "I can see that river from my office, you know."

"Yes, I do know."

Silence. The color that had been rising in his cheeks waned.

And for a gratifying moment, I let it. "Relax, Seth. I was just kidding. I can't imagine anything like that ever happening."

He didn't look convinced. Any assurance I offered in this unsettled pre-war climate would sound like lying. The tactic he usually took.

"Forget about it. Sorry I mentioned such a thing. What's really on my mind is a peninsula somewhere in Illinois. One my grandfather mentioned recently." Not merely mentioned, but insisted I visit.

It's in Mountain Grove, Illinois. That is what we called the town back then. Its real name is Grove. For all my stories, Jim, that is the one I never told you. It changed my life.

And Grandpa hoped it would change mine, but he didn't say that. Neither did I add that I doubted it would. I only told him I would do whatever he wanted. And I meant it.

Seth tensed. His eyes turned beadier behind his glasses. He always feared my life would need a change someday, whereas Grandpa knew it with certainty. He promised I would find my essence, the one difference between him and me, between his stories and mine, on his peninsula. He had looked so feeble, I preferred to stay close to him and write novels, leaving only to enlist someday and head overseas with either a gun as a soldier or my typewriter as a war journalist.

Type all the stories you want, son, but when you're ready to put life on a page, use this.

Seth truly would throw himself out his office window if I showed him the gold fountain pen my grandfather had given me at that moment. Seth paid me to write death, not life. Gruesome death I typed feverishly day and night. According to Grandpa, the pen had been handed down in our family, none of us ever using it. Not even him, a man of endless tales he loved to share—except for one. The one he wanted me to experience.

Someday, son, something will send your moral compass into a tailspin. Gravity will vanish, and you will fling your guards aside. What has always been singular vision will suddenly become kaleidoscopic. When that happens, grab this pen and write. With blood as your ink, write your heart on the page.

I couldn't imagine what Grandpa described ever happening to me, but the faraway glint in his eye suggested it had to him. Or at least he believed it had. He held the story close but pressed the pen in my direction. With his end seeming too near, I accepted the gold pen and agreed to go to Grove—or to Mountain Grove, as he called it. I would do it to honor him. Even though we apparently came from a long line of skinny, pensive, potential writers who never had their worlds dumped upside down, never confused right with wrong, and never felt our hearts enough to put them on paper with this particular instrument. He thanked me, the flicker in his eyes assuring me he had experienced every bit of what he described except for the writing part. Which he now bequeathed to me with the pen.

"I knew this would happen someday." Seth glared at contracts and manuscripts that meant far less to him than mine did. His lips vanished as he pinched them between his teeth. He was an unhappy family man who threw his all into the publishing world, and I was his main bread and butter. "Look." He swiped a growing sheen from his forehead. "How about a compromise? You do something for me if I let you go traipsing after some whim."

"It isn't a whim."

"Okay. Then before you go traipsing after some…something or other—I don't know what—you have to commit part of your time to me. You owe me that much, so tell me where this peninsula is located."

"In a small town called Grove, a little west of Chicago." Grandpa had marked it on a map. I would go, no matter what Seth said.

"I hoped you would say close to a big city. Chicago will work." He leaned to the side and rifled through a drawer, then plopped a file marked "*Times* Articles" on his desk's top.

I knew that folder well. Hoping to keep me stateside and profitable, Seth had offered my top-selling name as a contributor to them. The introduction had felt safe to him until the relationship swayed toward the new party, the *Times* calling the shots on my time and article content more and more. If this kept up, maybe someday I really would write about the body of an editor being dumped into the Hudson. A newspaper article instead of fiction. The harrowing account of a discarded third party when three became a crowd.

"I will agree to your compromise if I can write their

Randy Reed article. That guy was in Chicago, if I remember correctly, and his story was edgy." This was my crime-writer side talking, not the side with essence Grandpa wanted me to discover in Grove.

"You will write no such article." Seth kept the file close to him. "Too risky. That's why I turned it down when they first mentioned it. There is another suggestion in here about an enlisted man from Chicago who…"

"Reed is the only interview I will agree to." It appealed to me, but it would to Grandpa also. This was the perfect combination of terror and passion for us—a snitch exposing a love story that could get him and the two lovers killed. "If you want any say in my trip, call the *Times*. Get a meeting lined up with Reed if no one else has done the story."

"No one in their right mind would get anywhere near it." A sheen returned to Seth's forehead. "You think Hitler's going to sit quietly when he learns one of his own men slipped a Jewish woman out of one of his camps and escaped with her to the States?"

"My grandfather would call it the ultimate love story."

"The *Times* isn't looking for a love story. Neither am I, and I can't afford for you to go soft on me. Or get killed."

"No one who crosses Hitler, even with a typewriter, is soft. Call them. Now. I will make good on the interview, but the rest of my time will be my own."

Seth muttered something vile as he dialed his connection's number at the newspaper. This could turn out to be my usual typewriter job. A blood-and-guts story that would hopefully end well. Or it could present the opportunity to use the gold pen, since I expected

Grandpa's peninsula would do less for me than he hoped.

"The article is yours." Seth practically slammed the handset onto its cradle. He buried his face behind his hands but continued to talk. "The *Times* said to remind you this is only a tip. Don't write it as gospel."

Which meant even the king of newspapers was nervous.

"They will set up an interview with Reed and let us know when and where. Supposedly nothing has changed. Reed still claims Hitler's soldier took a fancy to a Jewish woman and snuck her out of the country right under his Führer's nose."

"Hitler's man, no matter how heinous he is, loved someone enough to risk his life for her." The sort of hero Grandpa spoke about. And the cunning mind I always wrote about.

"Cut the love stuff out. Stick to what you're good at. Anyway, the snitch with the story claims his name is Randy Reed. It's fake, we're certain, but go with it. He's scared." Seth dropped his hands to his desk. "Can't blame him. He won't live if either Hitler or the soldier who betrayed him finds out Reed leaked this story, even if it's all lies."

"And they might kill the messenger too. The one who tells the tale."

Seth looked as if his life was over because he feared mine might be. Ours was a strange relationship. I was more than his bread and butter—he had become fond of me. His glistening forehead buckled into worried furrows as I rose to my feet.

"Find me a hotel the pending war hasn't shut down or turned into something else yet, in or around Grove," I said and rapped my knuckles on one of the few bare spots on his desk. So I could find Grandpa's peninsula before writing about Randy Reed robbed me of the chance to ever learn what my grandfather never told me.

Chapter 2

I brought the gold pen along on my trip to Grove, though I would have preferred to bring Grandpa, my favorite traveling companion on book signings and interviews. He declined this time, and I didn't argue. Probably for the best, in case he saw what I expected to see—nothing. That whatever he treasured from years ago had been altered by time or modernization…or had never been there at all.

I unlocked the door of the hotel room Seth had found for me—actually, the *Times* had taken charge and secured it instead—and stepped inside. I glanced at the bedside table, the first thing I always did when Grandpa didn't accompany me. And there it was. A yellow envelope with his unmistakable cursive on the front. I smiled at "Jim" written in script so beautiful, I used to tease him about writing like a girl. "Thank you, Grandpa," I said to his way of being here when he wasn't. Something magical he always managed to accomplish, as if he sent his thoughts by carrier pigeon.

I closed a door too ordinary to keep out anyone tied to Hitler. If Reed turned out to be nothing but a glory-seeker, it wouldn't matter. After years of studying and writing about the criminal mind, I could detect a liar before he said a word. One look at Reed's eyes and how he positioned himself would tell me whether his story was fact or fiction. And whether or not I should ask for a room with more locks on the door.

The room looked and smelled freshly cleaned. Almost excessively so, as if someone scoured away everything I needn't see. Scanning the bare necessities in furnishings, I set my typewriter case beside the small desk and carried my suitcase to the bed. Grandpa's note, which would be on yellow paper that matched the envelope, wouldn't be his usual *Wish I was there,* or *Do your best work.* Not this time. Not in a town he called Mountain Grove instead of Grove.

Stripping off my hat and a jacket I didn't need in the warm June weather, I tossed them on the bed and opened my suitcase to a nest of clothing I peeled aside. From within its folds, I gingerly lifted a box of graying, veinous wood so old it was turning to dust. I carried Grandpa's treasure to the bedside table and set it beside his envelope.

Yellow is my favorite color, son. Someday it will be yours as well.

I doubted that. Even green and blue were too cheery for someone who made a living writing about murder. Removing the ancient box's lid, I brushed equally aged sawdust from the gold pen, but I didn't touch or remove it. That was for the day I found whatever story it was meant to write. Hopefully soon. Maybe. For Grandpa's sake, I prayed Grove offered up something.

"Mr. Turner?" A man called from outside my door following a soft knock.

"Yes?" I replied without opening it.

"A call for you, sir, in the main lobby."

From Seth, no doubt. He was more like a babysitter than an editor. Drat the invention that gave him a way to disrupt me no matter where I was.

"I will be right there." With the anticipation of opening Grandpa's note ruined, I left his envelope on the table and walked to a lobby which resembled my room—comfortably sterile. The hotel's neatly arranged fixtures were far less ornate than in others where I had stayed, Grove's unobtrusive and relaxing. I retrieved the handset of a telephone a rather starstruck clerk indicated across the lobby from the counter he stood behind. He clearly knew who I was. Maybe that was why my room seemed overly scrubbed. I mouthed a *thank you* to him as a voice shouted from the handset.

"Jim? You there?" I imagined Seth frowning at his telephone.

"Hello, and yes, I'm here."

"You found the hotel all right? It wasn't the one I chose for you, but…"

"Of course I found it. I'm here, and it is more than adequate. As I'm sure the one you picked out would have been also." If not for an admiring fan behind the counter, I would have burned Seth's ears with my annoyance at his call.

"Who would have thought a dinky place like Grove would even have one." Seth sounded more irritated than relieved. I could picture him in his office, New York City a cacophony of background noise he no longer registered. "So, you brought everything you need? Typewriter, paper, pencils?"

My typewriter remained on the floor in its case, where I intended to leave it for the time being. But Grandpa's pen, the original reason I came to Grove, was ready to go. "Everything is fine, Seth. Just let me know when Reed is ready to be interviewed." I lowered my voice for the last part, the clerk seeming to be all ears.

"Soon. Very soon, actually. The *Times* set it up in a hurry." The newspaper's rush and the edge to Seth's voice told me everyone expected Reed to end up dead. Hitler's long reach knew no obstacles, not even an ocean. His man who betrayed him would know that better than anyone.

"How soon?" I whispered with my back to the counter, praying Seth would say in three or four days.

"Tomorrow evening. Stick close to your room after five tomorrow. Reed is calling the shots, so be ready to go when you're told the time and place."

Reed's story was bringing the war closer to me than it had ever been. And bringing love with it as well, if Grandpa was right. Both more foreign than familiar, meaning I would quote my grandfather for the romantic elements—without citing him—in the article. "Will you be the one contacting me?" I asked.

"No. I'm out of the loop on this. The *Times* is playing this one close. You might get a call, or someone could pick you up at your hotel."

"You can tell your contact I won't get into a car with anyone. Reed isn't the only person allowed to call the shots."

My boldness shocked Seth. Maybe even the clerk, who cleared his throat behind me. It would force Seth to be equally bold with a newspaper he was growing to detest but cow-towed to. "Fine. Just be careful. I know you are ready for the interview, so go do something to distract yourself. Start your next story. Or series, even."

I had no intention of touching my typewriter until I had to. "We'll see. I will talk to you tomorrow, Seth." I hung up. If tomorrow could turn out as poorly as everyone feared, I had a peninsula to find today. I nodded my thanks to the clerk, again, who followed my exit with awe in his gaze.

Once in my room, I went straight to Grandpa's envelope. The way he scripted *Jim* filled the room with his voice and cleared Seth's from my head. I opened it and extracted his note.

The best stories are the true ones. They are fantasies when lived.

Grandpa's cursive further stilled the edginess my conversation with Seth had created. But what my grandfather said made little sense. I flipped the paper over.

Call me when you get in.

Whereas Seth drained me, Grandpa inspired me. Maybe a chat with him would point me in the right direction to unearth the fantasy he found in this ordinary little town. Grabbing my room key, I returned to the lobby and the clerk who hailed me as if I was royalty.

Grandpa was quick to answer when I called, and quick to respond to my first question.

"Yes, I lived a fantasy. For a brief time."

Which meant whatever happened in Grove had nothing to do with my grandmother, with whom he had spent years. Though I didn't write about moral dilemmas, my interest piqued. Had Grandpa married his second choice? Or were all fantasies only good for a moment? "Are you referring to living something like the crush I had on Robin West in high school?" I scrambled to at least try to understand.

He guffawed. "When you tripped over everything, gazed moon-eyed into space, and spent hours trying to manage your straight hair? As intense as that was, son, no. Not like that at all."

His breathing changed at the mention of his fantasy, but Robin's name had no effect on mine. "She clearly wasn't my fantasy." No one ever had been. "No wonder I kill characters rather than send them off in bliss."

Grandpa laughed again. "Do justice to the love story Reed will tell you when you write it, but more importantly, get out and take a walk. Explore the area."

He meant go find his peninsula. I gazed through the lobby's window and its glass door, wondering how I would tell him I found nothing worthy of his fantasy when we next spoke. Grove looked pretty ordinary from what I could see. A nearly empty parking lot and minimal traffic beyond. Certainly no mountain. Or anything fantastical which would warrant Grandpa's tightly held memory. "So, any clues as to what you found here?"

"A wonderful peninsula, for starters. And wherever there is a 'what' to find, also look for the 'who.' "

Grandpa and I both knew I had no antenna for the sort of person who could cause him to squeeze what felt like his eternity into a brief fantasy. Or the sort that could cause Hitler's man to risk torture and death for himself to avoid it for her. "I'll take a pad and pen with me. If nothing else, I will sit there and write."

"It isn't a pad and pen sort of spot." He paused. "It's the sort of place where a person breathes. Tastes. Experiences." He was no longer speaking my language. Certainly nothing I could write about.

"I will let you know what I find," I responded.

We said our goodbyes and hung up. Grandpa bore a poet's heart. Did my grandmother realize that? Or was she like me, touched by the storyteller's imagination and missing something of the man deeper inside? Whatever it was.

I corrected myself. *Whoever* it was. Because he said himself, where there is a "what" there is also a "who."

Chapter 3

Leaving my pen, paper, and typewriter behind, I set out on foot. Grove was small, too small to hide a lake large enough for a peninsula. I could find it before sunset, easily. Allowing me plenty of time to stand at its tip and wait for the experiences Grandpa claimed he had found.

Pausing in the hotel's parking lot, I pivoted, taking in a panoramic view of what I could see of this simple town. After a couple of unrewarding turns, my concerns grew and began to gnaw at my hope. Grandpa couldn't possibly have experienced anything fantastic in this place. Ordinary vehicles, average brick buildings, normal streets, large trees, even a tractor... My gut knotted in the absence of anything idyllic. What if this town's lack of stimulation caused Grandpa's poetic imagination to take over?

Determined to prove Grandpa all I believed him to be, I resisted the temptation to make short work of this project by asking the desk clerk if Grove even had a peninsula. Lifelong trust in my grandfather said to do this his way—walk and explore the area. Look for his "what" and "who."

"Okay, Grandpa." I shoved uneasiness aside and pondered which one of four possible directions I should take. Worry returned. If Grandpa had imagined a mountain, what if I found no peninsula? I could never tell him his fantasy was just that. A fantasy.

I chose a direction and made my way down the hotel's street past a short string of businesses. Beyond a vacant lot, the street changed to residential. The farther I went, the quieter the area became. Less affluent homes replaced average ones, until eventually older structures with poor upkeep became the norm. By the time I neared the town's edge, the houses shrank in size and bore little paint. They sagged as if something took their vibrancy out of them. I felt the same.

I looked around. No lake. Therefore, no peninsula in this direction. Nothing worthy of a story except for the eerie quiet which suited my tales. I raked a hand through my hair, and it fell back into its usual place. There were three more directions to look, and I would do that now. I refused to let Randy Reed's love story trump my grandfather's. Nor would I entertain the thought that the man who meant the world to me could be losing his mind. "Grandpa! Where is your story?"

"I have a story."

I wheeled around to a short and rather stout brown-haired woman wearing a frumpy outfit which might have been worn to do farm chores. Somewhere near my age and extraordinarily plain, her expression reminded me of a mother who knew her child would come around to her point of view if she waited long enough.

I didn't want her point of view or her story. "Do I know you?" Of course I didn't, but she might know me. A lot of readers recognized me, thanks to Seth. "I don't write for other people, if that is what you are hoping."

Instead of responding, she glanced upward and to my left.

I followed her gaze. My mouth fell open. A

weathered, wooden, two-story monstrosity I hadn't even noticed sat in a scrap of a yard next to where I stood. A ladder no one should trust stretched from the ground to an aged balcony with a railing as fragile-looking as the box that held Grandpa's gold pen.

"How did you know?" I asked without removing my gaze from a building that reeked of a whole new crime series. "If this is what you meant by a story, it is exactly what I needed." For this I would remove my typewriter from its case and set it up. I turned to the short woman. "Thank you." Could this be what Grandpa meant by a peninsula? Something metaphorical? This decrepit structure was already arousing the writer in me.

She said nothing, not even, "You're welcome." Maybe she wanted money for the rights to concoct tales about this building. "This place speaks to me, ma'am, but if it belongs to you, then I will happily…"

"You came." A sweet voice called from above.

I looked up. Straight into the face of an angel. Tall and slender, she leaned over the balcony railing. I gaped at the cutest young woman I had ever seen. I gaped even more when something yellow caught my eye. A yellow halo of loose blonde curls fluttered around her delightful face.

"You came," she said again and smiled. Glowed, more like it.

"Me?" I pointed at myself. "Or her?" Praying this beauty meant me, I gestured toward the short, brown-haired woman…who had vanished. I swiveled my head in every direction. She'd stood there seconds ago. Had I offended her?

"You, of course. Who else? Come on up." The blonde beckoned me to join her, this moment something like a scene from *Romeo and Juliet*. My heart rate kicked up.

"I would love to. I mean, I would like to." I considered the unpainted building that looked like something from the Old West. Did this girl need money? She was a stranger… For once maybe Seth was right when he warned me to be careful. "Actually, I should…"

"Please." She was so beautiful. Beautifully cute, her eyes enormous and blue.

"You don't even know me," I countered as I looked for a doorway on the lower level. I spotted none. "You can't invite strange men into your home. Well, I'm not strange, just a stranger."

"I know who you are." She gestured again for me to join her. "You are the perfect person to help me."

"Help you what?" With another story idea? Like the brown-haired woman had claimed to have? That I had failed to respond appropriately to once this blonde beauty caught my eye?

"Help me get ready for my wedding. I'm getting married three days from now." Her smile doubled in size. The one inside of me vanished.

"I have a schedule," I faltered. "Interviews and a book to write. Sorry. You have the wrong person." Though I wished she didn't.

"If you help me, I will help you. You be my hero, and I will be yours."

According to Grandpa, heroes loved someone or something. I was merely fascinated at this point. Maybe infatuated. Possibly lusting a little. "You hardly resemble the sort of heroes I write about, and I know nothing about weddings. Best we part ways now."

This gem of a girl belonged to some other guy. A

complication which had never been worth risking life or limb over before. Not even when Robin married our high school quarterback. But now my heart cavorted wildly merely looking at this beauty. Which meant I would never write about hoodlums again if I stayed around her for very long. This was a different sort of danger. Nothing like the kind I wrote about. I told my feet to walk away. I told my eyes to stop staring at her.

"The only way in is up?" I asked.

"It sure is. Come on." Her voice sang the invitation as she positioned herself near the ladder's top.

She was fetching. Irresistible.

And belonged to some other man, I reminded myself.

I grasped the ladder's splintery gray sides, ignoring the sharp pains, and set a foot on the bottom rung. Some beefy fiancé might well toss me back to the ground once I made it to the top.

"Here I come," I said foolishly. In a flash, I reached the top few rungs and paused. There was no heroic way to transition from the ladder to the balcony. My legs were long, but doing the splits between the upper rungs and the railing… I glanced down. "I'm glad men don't wear skirts."

"This way." The blonde sidled to where I should make my leap. No, she didn't sidle, she bounced.

"How?" I held onto the ladder for dear life.

She chuckled. "One leg at a time."

If she was younger than I, it wasn't by much, so surely I could match her strength and agility. I glanced down again.

"Don't worry," the beauty assured me. "I do it all the time, and I will help you."

For some reason, I trusted her. Boosted by her gaiety, I swung a leg to the railing, catching it with my ankle. "I will never make it." I did the splits from the ladder to where she beckoned me. "I can't do this."

"Yes, you can. You have to. Because I need you."

She needed me? "What about your…"

"My fiancé? Dwayne?" She grabbed me and pulled me by the back of my shirt until my calf made it over the railing. Then a knee, my pant leg bunching above my kneecap and exposing my skinny but hairy leg. Normally, writers weren't called upon for their muscle. Sweating profusely, even with her help and exhortations, I clumsily slithered over the rail and onto the balcony floor, landing on my back.

"You did it," she cheered above me.

Prostrate against worn boards, I gazed up at her grinning face and lovely yellow curls framed by the underside of the old building's eaves. "*We* did it," I corrected her.

"See? We need each other." The blue of her eyes intensified.

I swallowed at the pleasant sensation of needing each other. My Adam's apple exaggerated the effort. "My name is Jim, by the way."

"I know. You're Jim Turner, the writer, the answer to my prayers."

That would make the short, brown-haired woman who spoke to me at just the right moment an angel, and I sincerely doubted that. "I write mostly blood and guts, you realize."

"That's what makes you so perfect for me. You understand urgency, life-and-death situations. I'm so glad you were sent here."

"I wasn't really sent…" Well, I was if the glance upward by a complete stranger qualified. "Never mind. What is your name?" I struggled to a sitting position.

"I call myself Chastity."

"Call yourself?" I frowned at the most chaste expression I had ever seen on a young woman.

"Don't writers use pen names?"

"When we are hiding something."

Her lovely face reddened. "Just call me Chastity. Especially when my parents are around."

I sensed a story. I should have sensed it sooner, much sooner, maybe the moment the small, brown-haired woman appeared out of nowhere and claimed she had one. "What should I call the woman who was standing on the ground below earlier?"

"What woman?" Chastity leaned over the railing and looked down with a frown. "I didn't see anyone, and I still don't."

I scrambled to my feet. From this vantage point I searched every direction but saw no one along the sidewalks or standing in front of one of the nearby houses. I knew I hadn't imagined her. Grove was small. In a matter of time, I would run into the woman with the story again, or into someone who knew her.

"Won't you come in?" Chastity pointed to a door, evidently the only door to her living area. Two floors up and accessible by a ladder only a true Romeo could master.

"I doubt Dwayne would appreciate me being here with you." Not to mention her parents.

"Dwayne will be here three days from now."

"Three days? Isn't your wedding three days away?"

"He will make it." She seemed sure, yet his absence

resonated everywhere. He had staked a claim she held onto while he carried his part away.

Was I here to fill his shoes? Give her someone to share her excitement with until he returned? Or should I write him out of her story with lots of blood and gore?

"Come inside. You will love it here."

Exactly what I feared. I would love it here. Love her before three days were up because she was my exact opposite, the light to my dark writing moods, the fun to my agony of struggling with a story, the beautiful and brave heroine who dared to live in a building that looked as if it could collapse at any moment. Her blonde curls matched the yellow of my grandfather's envelopes. Her second-story apartment became Grove's mountain. One I wanted no one else to know about. And one I wanted to climb.

Chapter 4

As we stood there, I told myself to leave. I had a risky interview to conduct tomorrow evening and a new crime story to contrive. Not to mention, every time she smiled, my normally sharp edge softened. I would offer to buy Chastity whatever she needed for her upcoming wedding—with Dwayne—and escape.

The splintery door to her living area eased open in front of me, her lovely arm beckoning me to enter.

With no apologies to Dwayne, I did.

Chastity's home was awash with color, fabric, soothing fragrances, and cool breezes that swept around her cluttery arrangement of furnishings and me as I stood mesmerized by the oasis inside this stark building. Open windows without screens on either side of the front door, as well as the back one that stood ajar enough to expose another balcony, created a wind tunnel of delight.

"I didn't expect this." I took in an indoor panorama coordinated with all the organization of an artist's pallet. No system, no orderly arrangement of furniture, no color scheme, just beautiful chaos. If I stayed here too long, I really would end up writing mushy dime romance novels, just as Seth feared.

"You like it?" She dropped cross-legged on top of a pillow large enough to be a chair, looking like a child eager for my approval. "It's a little much, I know, but…well, it's me."

It was her. I didn't even know her, but it truly was her. Rows of three-foot-wide strips of fabric hanging from the ceiling to the floor flapped in the breeze, the only room divisions I could decipher. Loose rooms, fluid in design, as if transition without bearings was normal. Colorful pillows that didn't coordinate with her cloth walls were strewn everywhere. Nothing matched in this pastel mishmash of floral designs and soft patterns, yet it worked perfectly.

"Oddly, I do like it." I turned toward her grinning face, the blush of a bride, pure excitement for an upcoming life to which she was missing one important piece—her groom.

"Good." She rose from the pillow. "We have so much to do. You know how much work weddings are." She pinched her lips. "Well, you probably don't know. But you will."

Now it was my turn to blush. She probably hadn't read my books, but she certainly exhibited an uncanny knack for reading me. "If you mean because I've never married…" Or even dated with any frequency…

"It's okay." She came close. She smelled like her home, a wash of fresh breezes with a swirl of soft color. I wanted to cup that pretty face in my hands and stare at it forever. She patted my arm, more maternally than passionately, sending my fantasy out the window. "You can follow my lead. I know what to do. And… Wait. You're not in the middle of writing a book right now, are you?"

I was. This one. Everything else could wait. "I'm available," I lied to her worried expression and to myself. "Just tell me what to do."

"Wonderful!" She bounced on her toes, long legs

exposed beneath shorts far too short for current fashions. Pink shorts, instead of the bland fabric most often available due to a predicted war, dangled half hidden below a billowy shirt I could almost see through. "To start with…" Her voice broke my search for what I couldn't see. "We need to choose a place for the ceremony, design and send invitations, write an announcement for the newspaper, decide on cake and food, pick and arrange loads of flowers, finish my dress…"

"Wait. All of that? In three days?" I didn't know a thing about weddings, but I knew a well-executed assassination took more than three days to plan and pull off.

"See what I mean? So much to do."

"Do you have other people helping? Friends? Your mother?" Deadbeat Dwayne?

"Sadly, no. A couple of friends offered, but their free time is limited."

"So, I gather you have been engaged for only a short time."

Chastity laughed. "No, I've been engaged forever. When you know, you know, and that's how it was for Dwayne and me."

Then where was this object of Chastity's affection? If I were in her shoes, I would write him out of the story. And pencil me in…either as a fortuitous stranger or an answer to her prayer. An eager outsider, one intoxicated by her and her whimsical lifestyle.

And where had the two of them been during their "forever" engagement? What had they been doing instead of planning their wedding? "Three days. Okay. Where do we begin?"

"Don't worry, Jim. Three signifies completion. We have plenty of time."

Neither Chastity's math nor her philosophy made sense to me, but the lure of her excitement did. "Let's get started…even though we have plenty of time."

"Right. First of all, since you are a writer, would you compose a flowery announcement for the newspaper? You know, something that will make the heart go pitter-patter?"

Normally I stopped hearts in the stories I wrote. "Certainly. But to do that, we should include the location of the ceremony." Not to mention the groom.

"Right," she said again, then began to pace around her menagerie of colorful objects. For the first time, I noticed a collection of bracelets jangling around both of her wrists—beads, tiny pearls, and charms created a cacophony of clatter and glimmer. My gaze traveled up her long arms to the bodice of the loose shirt which fluttered in the breeze as she zigzagged through her home. "Dwayne prefers the outdoors. And I have always loved gazebos." She tapped her lips as she continued her trek.

As if I knew what I was doing, I considered the time of year and pondered the types of flowers currently in season. Then I smacked my forehead. Here I was, Jim Turner, renowned author of suspense, plotting greenery suitable for tender nuptials instead of a mass murder. "I don't think I'm going to be much help…"

"Oh, Jim." She darted to me, gripped my arms, and pinned me with her large blue eyes. "You are perfect for this job. Your books prove how good you are at planning and executing a scheme. I have three days. Who better than you to pull this off?"

Dwayne came to mind. "No one," I said instead. If my talent was enough for her, those blue eyes were enough for me.

"Okay, good. Now..." She let go of my arms and paced again. "We will have the wedding at Shale Lake. There is no gazebo there, but Dwayne loves that place. He will be thrilled when he finds out."

"Which will be..."

"When he gets here three days from now."

As a master of suspense, I caught the subtle tautness of her response, a shadow on everything jovial I relished about her. I kicked myself for inferring the man who would miss three days of excited planning would also fail to be at her side for their wedding.

"We will be ready by then, and he will be happy," I heard myself say to restore her glow. Then further surprised myself by realizing I almost meant it. Chastity was beautiful, but even more so when she bubbled with excitement. I wanted that for her. No matter what it cost me in the end. "Should we go look at Shale Lake and decide exactly where the wedding will be?"

"No, not yet. First, write the announcement. We will drop it off at the newspaper on our way to the lake. Just say something like, 'A trail of rose petals will mark the ceremony's location,' but in reality, we will post signs." She grinned.

I kicked myself for darkening her gaiety earlier. I would cast no more aspersions regarding her missing fiancé. After all, who was I? We were complete strangers.

"All right then..." I glanced around her chaos for a typewriter...or paper...maybe a pen.

"Can you write in here?" she asked. "I've heard

writers are finicky about where they create their stories."

She was right. I did my best work in a stark room with beige walls and no decorations, a single bulb hanging from the ceiling. No distractions. Just a writing desk and a typewriter. "For what you want written, I had best stay here."

She rifled through pillows, fabric-covered boxes, scarves, and whatever else got in her way, searching for a pen and paper. By the time she unearthed what I would need, I knew exactly what I would say about this gem of a girl whose forehead now glistened from exertion. Resisting the temptation to graze her hand, I took the pen and paper from her.

"Here's what I think you should say." She plied me with highlights of her romance with Dwayne, their chance encounter and the immediacy of their commitment, their starry optimism for the future.

I couldn't write that way. I didn't take dictation. I always plotted with my head and wrote from the gut. But this time, I wrote from the heart, penning my vision of Chastity's awakening into the passion which oozed from her and all around her home.

"Did you get all of that?" she stopped and asked.

"That and more," I assured her. Though I had captured her enthusiasm on the page, not a single one of her words made it there. Not even their full names. I referred to them as Chastity and Dwayne, and nothing more. I believed the universe already recognized her, this beautiful explosion of life and color in a world darkened by war. Dwayne carried the distinction of the one lucky enough to orbit her as long as they both should live. I choked down my objection to that and forced a smile.

"Good. Let's go then. Shale Lake isn't far. We will

take our bicycles. Mine and Dwayne's, but go to the newspaper first."

I imagined a bicycle too short for me as she led me to an out-of-the-way place beneath the side balcony…or I hoped it would be too short. Tall and lanky, I envisioned myself towering over her missing fiancé.

"We can lower the seat on Dwayne's bicycle if you need to." She eyed me up and down. "You are tall, but he is really tall."

I tried not to gasp at a seat Dwayne surely had custom made, the post it sat on longer than any I had ever seen.

"This should suit me just fine," I lied. What was this guy? A grandaddy longlegs?

Chastity's bicycle was the picture of her and her living arrangement—flowers, a large pink basket on the handlebars, its paint job irregular splotches of color. She grinned and rang its bell as I struggled to throw a leg over Dwayne's seat without toppling over.

Once I'd straddled the middle bar, I stood and pumped the whole way in spite of Chastity's insistence I sit and coast whenever possible. Rather than admit Dwayne's legs were longer than mine, I assured her I preferred my upright position. And vowed to myself to add a character no one liked to my next novel. A hoodlum named Stick who wouldn't live longer than a chapter.

Because Grove was so small, we managed to pedal to and from the newspaper office in a matter of minutes.

"Did you think the society page editor was a little put off by the length of the announcement you wrote?" Chastity pedaled pensively from the newspaper office toward the lake, her slower speed making it difficult for me to keep my balance.

"Trust me, they will love it."

A grin creased the side of her face I could see. "Good." With that, she sped up.

The lake's surface glimmered through trees as we left the edge of town. Chastity expertly steered us to an opening which formed an entrance, a grassy roadway dotted by tiny gravel which took us to the lake's edge. "The water is so blue," I said when we stopped, horrifying myself, my normal thoughts about any scenery being where one could hide a body. "I mean…"

"Oh, I know what you mean." She latched onto my arm. Straddling our bicycles, we stood side by side drinking in an aquatic scent heavier than rain, and feeling the breeze as it swept the water's surface into a frenzy of sparkles. Sparkles? What was happening to me? "There is a slight peninsula over there." Chastity pointed.

My mouth gaped. I think my face paled. Grandpa wasn't losing his mind after all.

"I know. It is surprising," she said, smiling at my astonished expression. "Who would have thought a lake this small would have such a gorgeous peninsula? There is a picnic shelter on it, making it the perfect place for a wedding. What do you think?"

All I could think was, it had to be Grandpa's peninsula. Did he meet some blonde-headed girl there, resulting in his love of yellow? "It all suits you. The green grass, blue sky, fresh air…" I wanted to thump my head. Seth would, if he could hear my dreamy babbling.

"It suits Dwayne too. This is why you are the perfect person to help me. You see exactly what I see."

"It will be windy," I added an intentional damper on Dwayne's taste. When she frowned, I inwardly kicked myself. "I mean, it might be windy. So if you plan to serve food out here, everything will need to be anchored down."

"Oh. Good point. We can make cupcakes instead of a big cake. No meal, no plates or utensils." She looked hopeful.

"Problem solved." I tried to restore her from the darkness I had caused. Again. Maybe negativity came naturally with a personality that wrote crime. And violence. And now I could add jealousy to my scandalous specialties. "Look, maybe I'm not the right person to help you. I mean, don't you think it strange that I'm here? You really don't even know me."

"I know you, James Allan Turner. Everyone knows you. Stop being modest. I recognized you the first moment I laid eyes on you, and like I said, you are the answer to my prayer."

Then I needed to behave more like one. "Okay. I will see about reserving this peninsula. Show me your guest list later and we will send invitations and figure out how many cupcakes are needed. And who can bake them for you. Quickly."

"That would be my mom." Chastity gazed across the water, her eyebrows knitting together. "She bakes. She also wants the whole wedding and reception to be held at their church. The one my father pastors."

"Your father is a preacher?"

"Not in Grove, but in a smaller town not far from here. They call him Pastor Hugh. Hugh and Ruth Higgins." Her lower lip protruded slightly. "I wish I could use their church. But I can't." She laid a hand over her midsection slightly below her waist.

I stared until I caught the significance of her hand

placement, the protective embrace of what typically grew in that area. "Oh," I muttered. My heart sank. This beautiful creature truly did belong to Dwayne. Who didn't deserve her. What sort of hero left his heroine to face judgmental masses on her own in her condition?

"Is it a God rule or man's rule that you can't marry in their church?" I wouldn't take God on, but I would defend her from man. Since her fiancé didn't.

"Neither." Her smile was wan. "I just can't let my parents know about..." She patted her tummy. "It would hurt them to learn that I..."

I raised a hand. Neither did I want to learn about or envision what she and Dwayne had done. I couldn't bear the image of moments in his arms which made her feel they had been engaged forever. "Then it will stay our little secret." One I wouldn't talk about for her sake or think about for mine.

"Thank you." She sidled closer with her bicycle and leaned her head against my upper arm, her disarray of curls tickled the skin below my shirt sleeve. Was that lemon I smelled? I tipped my head toward hers and took a whiff. Most girls wore noxious perfumes, flowery enough to burn the nostrils. But lemon... I inhaled deeply.

"Have you ever been in love, Jim?"

Besides right this moment?

"You don't have to answer. I know men don't enjoy talking about feelings, but I'm sure you have been. How could someone like you never have tasted such delicious passion?" She looked up. "I hope you didn't get your heart broken, but I bet you have broken many a young girl's heart."

Before I could conjure a lie, she straightened her

bicycle. "We will invite twenty people to the wedding, but only seven will come. My parents, Dwayne's mother and sister, and three friends."

I wondered about the others when she began to pedal toward the peninsula. "We will still provide enough food for twenty people," I said as I caught up with her.

"You are so thoughtful, Jim. And thank you. But they really won't come." She said it with such wispy finality, I didn't argue. But I wondered who in their right mind could resist an invitation from a girl like Chastity? Certainly not thirteen people I would invite. I had three days to learn who they were and why.

I pedaled behind her as she continued toward the peninsula, captivated by her slender form, her cloud of curls, and her lemony scent.

My God, what was happening to me? I came to Grove to write what might be the final words of a man Hitler or his ex-soldier would surely come after. And I came to find Grandpa's...

Suddenly we were there. Chastity wheeled her bicycle onto a tree-covered finger of land that pointed into a blue-and-diamond-colored lake. We entered the grove of trees, followed a sort-of path between them, passed a quaint, low-walled shelter, and came to a stop where land ended and water began.

The lap of the waves on the peninsula's banks turned to words, speaking a language I had never heard before—the sounds of eternity, support, and surety. Water, the ground, and trees bolstered this peninsula and anyone who chose to stand here and listen.

Side by side, Chastity and I straddled our bicycles once again. She took my hand, her fingers tangling through mine and sending a euphoric sensation up my arm to places where feelings like that had never been. Which meant when we left this magical spot, I had to put an end to this. Tell her I had a book to write, an interview to do, and wish her the best.

"Thank you, Jim," she sighed.

At the tip of Shale Lake's peninsula, the breeze wrapped itself around Chastity and me the way our fingers wound around each other's. "Mountain Grove," I whispered, feeling my grandfather...and maybe someone else...all around us.

"Mountain Grove?" Chastity cast me a quizzical look, her face even cuter when she scrunched it.

"Something my grandpa called this place." How could I explain what I didn't understand?

"Mountain Grove." She repeated it as if she was tasting it. I watched her lips work the words before they puckered pensively. "I would like your grandfather."

And he would like her. I nodded and looked away, across water that shimmered toward us. Where Chastity and I stood truly was the perfect spot for a wedding. I felt it. I knew it to the core of my being.

Someday something will send your moral compass into a spin. Gravity will vanish, and you will fling your usual guards aside. What has always been singular vision will suddenly be kaleidoscopic. That is when you grab this pen and write. With blood as your ink, write your heart on the page.

Today was my someday. And standing beside her became my something.

Chapter 5

I floated back to my hotel at the end of the day, memories of Chastity and Grandpa's peninsula keeping my feet off the ground and my normally practical mind somewhere up in the clouds. I understood now what my grandfather had meant years ago, that an eternity could be encapsulated into a brief amount of time. And how that short-lived experience could become like a fantasy and last forever. A place where the lines between the real and the surreal became blurred.

"Mr. Turner? Sir?"

The sound of my name momentarily cleared my blissful cloud, and I found myself inside the hotel lobby, soft lamplight around me, and behind me a closed door I had no recollection of walking through. Evening had come. The end to a day of euphoria. I tried to focus on the clerk standing behind the counter, the night clerk, apparently, his rather round face looking more so between the flat brown cap and high-buttoned matching jacket. "I'm sorry. You were speaking to me?"

"Sir, a number of messages accumulated while you were out today." He swept away from the counter without explaining how it was he recognized me, an assortment of notes splayed like a poker hand in his fingers. "They're all from the same person. He said it was urgent."

Urgent seemed unimportant when viewed from

somewhere above the earth. Unless... "Not from my grandfather, I hope."

"They are from someone named Seth. He never gave his last name, but he claims to be the one paying for your room. He mentioned that several times when neither I nor the day clerk could account for your whereabouts."

"My apologies. And I guarantee you, it is nothing urgent. Seth is my editor, and he has a flair for the dramatic." When I took hold of the notes, the clerk held them tight. "Is there something else?"

"I'm sorry." He released them. "Except, I was wondering..."

"If you could have an autograph?"

"Yes. Please." He darted behind the counter and returned with a stack of books, a dozen at least, pinned between his hands and his double chin. "Several autographs, actually."

Was this how it happened to Grandpa? One minute he was in heaven, living his fantasy, then suddenly he was back on earth? The euphoria gone? Life and marriage replacing it?

"Of course..." I eyed his name tag. "...Wally. I would be happy to." I smiled at a man who, like me, might be pondering an enlistment which would take him overseas away from his life in the States. We both lacked the typical soldier physique, he being short, round, and slightly older with less hair, if I could judge by the sprigs showing below his cap. According to Seth, I was doing my part by distracting people on the Homefront from the vulgarities of war. Wally maybe felt his part was to help keep this hotel operating smoothly. My pre-Chastity author persona carried Wally's books to a nearby sofa and coffee table, but my new wedding-announcement-writer took over. "Tell me who I am signing these for, and I promise to make it good."

Wally grinned. So did I. Seth's urgency was forgotten as I signed books and Wally rattled on about my varied story plots in a way that sounded like he had taken a course on them rather than merely enjoyed them. Chastity's lemony scent lingered, adding zest to my signature, her heavenly, misty presence daunted only by Wally's alphabetical recounting of my heroes and villains. When finished, I handed a slightly sweaty Wally his signed books and returned to my room. And to uninterrupted reflections of Chastity.

Kicking the door shut behind me, I glanced at Seth's notes as I walked to the dresser. "Call me now" was written on each one…minus the exclamation points Seth's tone likely warranted. I wouldn't call him now. I couldn't. Discussing Randy Reed or murder would be impossible while pastels, blue eyes, and breezes lingered around me. Seth would detect Chastity's impact in a moment and torment the hotel desk clerks even more with endless phone calls.

Setting the notes aside, I looked into the dresser's large mirror and studied my reflection. It could have been my grandfather's at the time he visited Grove, we were so much the same. Possibly even down to the slight flush on my cheeks—the rosy hue of living and not just being alive.

"Get a grip on yourself," I admonished my image, then reddened more as I recalled signing Wally's books with the same fanciful flair my grandfather wrote with. "You are Jim Turner." I struggled for that pensive writer's look Seth encouraged. "This time tomorrow, you will be interviewing a man who may never be seen again." I rubbed my cheeks with the heels of my palms. I couldn't interview Reed with a flush of happiness on my face. Somehow I had to help Chastity without coming away from her with a rosy glow. My skin burned and I rubbed harder.

"Mr. Turner?" Wally's voice came from outside my door.

With a final glance at cheeks more flushed than ruddy, I went to the door and flung it open.

"Are you all right, sir?" Wally seemed taken aback as he eyed a face much redder than he had seen moments ago.

"I am. I was. I presume Seth has called again?"

"No, sir. It's a woman. She is…"

"A woman?" Not even the heroes in my books moved with the speed I did. "Thank you." I rushed past Wally, slamming my door closed, and bolted for the lobby. And Chastity. Whatever she needed, I would give her. Whatever she wanted was hers.

Skidding to a halt outside the lobby's door, I composed myself, steadied my breathing, then pushed through it to the cluster of sofas and chairs and scoured the area for her blonde curls and blue eyes. Nothing. Maybe Wally meant she had called. I wheeled toward his telephone, the handset nestled in its cradle where it belonged. No Chastity. No call.

"Mr. Turner?" The voice was husky, but unmistakably a woman's. She rose from one of the chairs as I turned, her form a solid rectangle that even her plain belted dress didn't add any femininity to. "Mr. Turner." Abandoning her previous courteous address, she clearly knew who I was. Lots of people recognized me. But I could tell, by the expressionless look on a face which seemed hardened rather than softened by age, this was no fan of my fiction. Perspiration dampened my collar.

Wally entered the lobby and sidled around us, stopping behind the counter. I wanted to join him, to escape this woman's dour demeanor that darkened my newfound elation.

"May I help you?" I asked her instead. Maybe the hair severely pulled back from her face fixed her features in their rigid positions.

"Is there someplace we could talk?" She probably meant somewhere safe from Wally's ears. Or from those of the man who lingered in another of the lobby's chairs, his face hidden behind a newspaper.

I gestured outside, and she frowned. She apparently didn't wish to be seen publicly as much as she didn't want to be overheard privately. But under no circumstances would I invite her to my room. I gauged her to be the darker side of forty and, though dressed like a woman, she was built like a rock. The opposite of Chastity... Chastity! Every choice I made could affect her.

"Outside," I commanded, refusing to waver. Not waiting for an argument or a response, I pushed through the door into the evening's dusky shade, instantly regretting my decision. My goodness. Just one afternoon with a woman like Chastity had dulled my keen edge. Even my characters knew better than to meet a stranger alone in the dark. "Right here is fine." I stayed near the light glowing from the lobby's glass door as the tank of a woman joined me.

She immediately utilized a tactic I employed in my stories—silence. It loosened every tongue. Except mine. My collar grew moister, but I said nothing as I waited for her to crack.

"I have a message for you," she said at last.

My breathing changed and my face warmed. Two more things which would get me killed in one of my books. "From whom?"

She ignored my question. "You are being watched."

Before I could utter a response, she disappeared. Even with her bulk, she strode with purpose and vanished into the dark.

"What do you mean? Who sent you?" I shouted too late into the darkness where she had vanished. I was being watched? Who was watching me? Randy Reed? Hitler? Dwayne? After a hasty glance around, I hurried back inside the lobby and went straight for the telephone under Wally's steady gaze.

With the phone cradled against my ear, I dialed Seth's number with one hand and slid the other down my face, the rhythmic rotary sound failing to soothe me.

"This better be you, Jim," Seth barked into my ear when he picked up.

"It's me. Hello to you, too."

"About time." His gruffness transformed into a near shout. "It scared me to death when I couldn't reach you. Warren, or whatever the hotel clerk called himself, was no help."

"Wally," I corrected him. "Big fan of mine, so be nice." Hunkering close to the phone, I gave Wally a smile over my shoulder.

"Right. Wally. Where in the world have you been?"

Where I had been seemed distant and otherworldly. "I found my grandfather's peninsula, but that's not why I called."

"I don't like you chasing after your grandfather's

fancies. Especially not before a risky interview I wasn't in favor of to begin with. You're the one who insisted on talking to Reed, so you need to keep your edge."

As usual, Seth's world's-eye-view was narrowed to what mattered to him only. To remind him I came to Grove for myself but agreed to do the interview for him and the *Times* would translate to nothing more than that I had a job to do—for him in particular. He would fall apart if I dared to mention my promise to assist in the arrangement of a wedding.

"You will be no match for anyone hunting Reed down," Seth ranted on.

Which meant putting myself in danger put Chastity at risk as well.

"It won't be Hitler who is after Reed, by the way. He won't care about that snitch beyond how bad the story makes him look. Hitler will be after the one who betrayed him. Which means the moon-eyed deserter is who Randy needs to worry about. You do too."

I saw myself in shoes identical to Randy's. Two men hindering the love affairs of other men. Dwayne's in my case. Surely far less dangerous than stepping into the involvements of someone trained by Hitler.

"We're talking about a crime of passion over a crime for dominance," Seth barged on. "A crime of passion turns Fifi the lapdog into a snarling wolf. Personally, I would rather cross a man defending his cause over one protecting his lover."

I swallowed audibly. Seth might be referring to men who were powerful on a global scale, but his description fit my Grove conundrum. Chastity was Dwayne's lover. Her yellow curls, her blue eyes, the near fantasy way she lived, all belonged to him. And here I was, beyond enthralled with her. Smitten. More than smitten, if I was honest.

I nibbled my lower lip as I weighed my opposing passions of fear versus ravenous longing. The latter quickly won out, creating an urge to betray my editor and coerce Chastity to ditch Dwayne. We could escape her Hitler—Dwayne—and my czar—Seth.

"Keep your focus, Jim. Stay away from that peninsula." Seth's sharp tone struck like a slap in the face.

Focus. Chastity would never leave Dwayne. Her devotion to stick with him matched mine to protect her. The passion which had envisioned the two of us fleeing together dwindled. I recouped my prior resolve to protect her and what mattered to her. No matter what the cost.

"Someone is watching me." I rallied my senses that understood danger.

Seth remained quiet for a moment. "Probably the *Times*," he finally said.

"What?"

"Yeah, they sent someone there to keep an eye on you."

A chilling reminder that even they were nervous. "You mean, one of their own people told me they were watching me? Shouldn't they have phrased it that they were looking out for me? Something positive and reassuring?" This didn't make sense. Why the secrecy? Why not ask Seth to tell me? "Also, if it was them, they sent a woman. Not even a young and able-bodied one." As tough as she looked, that woman couldn't do much more than watch while I got pummeled.

"Actually, that's pretty savvy of them," Seth said. "An older woman won't catch anyone's attention. A young knockout would. And a young man would certainly put someone who had been trained by Hitler on alert."

Seth rambled on while I lingered at "knockout." He was right. Men noticed women like that, women like Chastity. Suddenly, my thoughts flew to what might have happened years ago to my grandfather on the peninsula and to someone with him. Someone with hair so blonde it seemed yellow. Or who wore yellow ribbons. Yellow something… What could have been a lifetime of pleasure for them turned into a brief fantasy. Because Grandpa sacrificed what he wanted in order to protect her somehow. With passion equal to what Hitler's deserter must have felt when he slipped the woman he loved out of Europe.

A heroic call rose up inside of me. A hero's heart I had never experienced before surpassed my power to cunningly craft a plot. The fervency to protect who or what meant the most to me outdid my abilities at cerebral hijinks.

Heroes aren't heroes because they are clever or brave, but because they love someone or something deeply.

"My grandfather was so right," I murmured.

"What?" Seth's tone sharpened.

"Nothing."

"Your grandfather is anything but nothing. He frightens me, actually. I never quite understood him." Seth couldn't possibly understand him. My editor belonged to our publisher, not to the wife he'd briefly mentioned once, and whom I had never seen. Seth's heart pumped dollar signs, not ardor.

I glanced over my shoulder for the woman, but only

saw a family distracting Wally at the counter. All these years writing for Seth, I had missed the greatest story never told. The one at Grandpa's peninsula—a true hero giving up everything for the sake of the woman he loved.

"Don't worry, Seth, my grandfather likes you." The man who had been reading a newspaper was now gone. I scoured the room. How had he escaped without my notice?

"I doubt it. But anyway, let's hope Reed turns out to be a liar and this story never goes to press. Not even as a plot in one of your books. But until we know for certain, put everything else on the back burner. You need to be sharp tomorrow evening. Focus." He barked the last word with enough fervor that the family at the counter turned. I smiled and waved. But Seth was right. Spending tomorrow with Chastity could cost me dearly in the evening. Worse than that, it could cost her also.

"Okay. I will. But before I let you go, what were you calling me about that was so urgent all day?"

"What? Oh, that. Since I knew you would traipse off after your grandfather's notions, I thought it wise to line up another interview. One that would keep your crime-writing side sharp."

"No, not on this trip…"

"Especially on this trip. This interview isn't for the *Times*, it's for you. There's an ex-con in Chicago named Clyde. Really bad guy who loves boasting about his brutal insight into the criminal world. His rap sheet supposedly makes the skin crawl. I thought you should talk to him."

"No."

"I already set it up. I will give you the details after you interview Reed."

"My crime-writing skills are as sharp as ever," I lied. "So cancel Clyde. And goodnight. I'm going to bed now."

"We'll discuss the ex-con later. Get plenty of sleep. And bolt your door."

I would take Seth's last piece of advice. We hung up and I returned to my room, not a soul in sight as I went. Once locked inside, I set my typewriter's case on the small desk to ready it for tomorrow. It felt lighter than usual. Had Seth's worst nightmare happened, and it ran out of crime-fighting words? If so, he would kill me before anyone else got the chance. Opening the case's lid, I set my typewriter into its place, checked the ribbon, then rolled a clean page into the bail. To bolster the Jim Turner who sometimes wrote for the *Times*, I took a seat in front of it.

But thought about Chastity.

The sheet of paper remained clean and wordless all night, not even a title suitable to Reed's story came to mind. The only ideas that occurred to me were ones best written with Grandpa's gold pen. Did this mean my crime-writing days were gone?

Chapter 6

I dunked myself into a tub of hot bathwater after a sleepless night. Then, like a sea mammal breaking the ocean's surface, I emerged the moment I realized Grandpa would have my answer. He could either tie or untie the knot between the Grove where I had an interview to conduct and the Mountain Grove which made me want to live the relationship Reed intended to expose. After all, it was Grandpa's gold pen, his peninsula, his story that he kept to himself all these years, which brought me here. Not to mention his tales of heroes and their dedicated hearts, tales he had dropped like breadcrumbs my whole life, marking the path I now found myself on.

Grabbing a towel, I swiped it over my body, then used it as a comb to rearrange hair that would do what it wanted to anyway. Once dressed, I hurried to the hotel lobby where yesterday morning's clerk greeted me.

"Mr. Turner." He looked pleased to see me. The way a fan of my books normally looked at me. Admiring, but from a respectful distance. Unlike his coworker, Wally, from the night before.

"I need to use the telephone…Kevin…" I replied to his polite offer of help as I read his nametag. Then I stopped before hurrying to the phone. Maybe someone who was too admiring and disrespectful of personal distance could be of use and provide me with some information. "Actually, there is something else. The night clerk...Wally..."

"Don't know much about him, sir. He's new." He rapidly dismissed his coworker. Had whatever trait that caused Wally to memorize and recite my characters annoyed this man somehow?

"I see. Sorry to have bothered you." I hurried to the public phone as Kevin busied himself, looking down at the counter instead of at me. Maybe I didn't want to know when Wally next worked, or if he knew anything about the woman who had asked for me the night before.

My grandfather picked up after the first ring. "Hello, son."

"How did you know it was me?" He always knew, but I asked anyway.

"The phone rings a little differently when it's you." He chuckled. The same way he did when he told me my knock at his door was distinctive while growing up.

The sound of his throaty laugh made me wish I were there—twelve years old again and sitting cross-legged on the floor in front of his chair, listening to his stories. Absorbing the wisdom he threaded through each one. Never once dismissing his subtle revelations about a man's soul, which I now desperately wished I had paid attention to.

"Things are kind of strange here." My face warmed at such a feeble introduction to what was bothering me. No wonder my typewriter page remained blank all night.

Grandpa was a good listener. Never one to approach my problems like a handyman in a hurry to fix something, he remained quiet.

"I have my interview with Reed tonight, the guy everyone worries won't survive once the story hits the press. And Seth found a gangster he wants me to meet…"

"Because he's worried you might do something which will cost him his star crime writer. Like falling in love. That's your real question, isn't it?"

The phone's handset slipped from my grasp. It bounced off the small table, then spun in dizzying circles as it dangled by its cord.

"Is everything all right, sir?" Kevin called as my thoughts twirled with the receiver.

"No. I mean, yes." I gave him a weak wave and recovered the handset. "I dropped the phone," I apologized to my grandfather, hoping he wouldn't…or maybe would…ask why.

"For all the mountains a man faces, the biggest is the mountain inside him. We all come to it at some point."

"Is that the reason I'm in Mountain Grove?"

"There is no Mountain Grove. That's just what we called it."

"Who is we?"

" 'We' is the ink in the gold pen, Jim. Without 'we' a story is just thoughts."

Type all the stories you want, son, but when you're ready to put life on a page, use this.

The gold pen he referred to.

My head spun with questions I couldn't slow down. Did Grandpa see the mountain in me, which I only vaguely sensed? Did I really need to know about it? Could I type interviews and stories, but write life with the pen as well? Should I mention Chastity? Or just leave Grove and Mountain Grove behind and return to my old life in New York before it was too late?

"My writing is blocked," I said.

Grandpa's small smile was audible, a sympathetic and knowing silence I had seen and felt a million times. "That's what mountains do."

I waited for some advice, a "keep climbing" cliché, a boost for me to scale the impossible so my words would come back even better than before. Instead, he merely said he had to go. Which meant I should as well. But where? Upward? Forward? Back home without even talking to Reed? Seth would hunt me down.

As soon as I hung up, Kevin's phone began to ring.

"Don't answer that until I'm outside," I told him. "Then tell Seth I'm gone." Grandpa was right about a telephone's ring. The one jangling the phone off the counter rang with Seth's urgency. I hurried outside to my car. By the time I reached it, I knew where to go.

Shale Lake shimmered through the trees as I approached. The same way it had when Chastity first brought me here. I pulled my car into the lot, parked, and left it there. How could my grandfather say so much and so little at the same time?

In a matter of minutes, I reached Grandpa's peninsula and its grove of trees that I trudged through to the land's tip, where I stopped. Water lapped the toes of my shoes as I became a bridge between its sheen and the ground I stood on. Grandpa's Mountain Grove happened to him on this peninsula. Was that what was happening to me? In three days the first girl I had ever fallen for would marry another man. Right here. Their feet where mine stood now. Not even Hitler made me shudder as much as that did.

I faded back from the water's edge and sank down onto the grass. Knees up, I rested my chin on arms I folded across their tops. A soft breeze swept the scent of damp earth, soaked rocks, and glistening waves in my direction.

Minutes moved like hours as I immersed myself in the setting that had changed my grandfather's life. As I breathed, tasted, and experienced the peninsula the way he said I should, Shale Lake's shimmering surface became a screen where my life played in slow motion, a monochromatic and monotonal series of events with no plot and few highlights. Until Chastity…

Time stopped then, and Seth's fears became mine. What if I had fallen in love? Could that happen in less than a day? Or was I merely intoxicated by her colorful world, her quirky style, her large blue eyes and cute expressions? Would real love dare to take her away from her fiancé? Or would it spend three divine days in her presence and then walk away.

My new heroic side sprang up once again, a passion to be and do good for her. My baser nature countered with another type of passion that yearned to be with her. One side of me would scale the mountain, the other would tunnel beneath it.

I chose the high road. I would love Chastity by doing what was best for her. My brand new heroic side could manage that for three days.

"Yes," I shouted my charge to the lake as I stood and then turned. And looked into blue eyes surrounded by curly blonde locks. "Chastity…"

My heart hammered. My baser nature struck up a celebration at my instantly weakened resolve.

"I thought I might find you here," she said as she approached.

My heroic side faltered.

Heroes aren't heroes because they are clever or

*brave, but because they love someone or something
deeply.*

Heroes give. They don't take. The closer she came,
the more I wanted to take. *No*, I hissed inwardly as she
came near.

Her adorable expression pinched with concern when
she stopped in front of me. "You look awful, Jim. Didn't
you sleep well?"

My raging battle waned. "It's just some writing
issues…"

She rested her hand on my shoulder and stretched
closer for a better look, bringing her lemony scent with
her. "I must be wearing you out. Of course I am. No
wedding talk this morning. Instead, I have just the thing
to restore you. Come with me to my house." The wind
swept her blonde curls around her face, her eyes full of
remorse and worry. What sort of fiancé would leave a
girl like this behind? What sort of writer would?

She took my hand. A teeny voice inside my head
warned me not to fall in love with this girl. Once at my
car, I loaded her bicycle in the trunk and drove us to her
ramshackle house. I parked and tried to compose myself.

"Come inside," she said from the passenger seat.

I couldn't fall for a girl whose wedding I promised
to help plan. I climbed out of my car and glanced over its
top at her balcony, her open door and windows where
fabric walls and curtains billowed out with the breeze.
This wasn't a home. It was heaven.

My inner war returned. "It's just three days. How
much damage can occur in such a small amount of
time?" my dark and selfish side reasoned. "Enough to
cost both of you dearly if you don't get a grip on
yourself," my shinier side countered. "What's three

days? What could go wrong in seventy-two hours?" my dark side persisted. My shiny side considered the matter settled. "It's who it could go wrong *for* that matters."

"Jim." Chastity's voice floated from the car window.

My heart hammered at the sound of my name from her lips, and my dark side raised another victory shout. I rushed to open her door. Chastity's smile joined mine as she exited, and we walked toward her ladder where the wind would carry us upward…

"Focus," I whispered as we crossed a yard void of grass, an absolute contrast to the color and vibrancy that awaited us above. I took hold of the ladder's side and paused.

"You help me, and I will help you." The cutest young woman I had ever seen stood at the ladder's opposite side. She offered me a pact that would end after three days—two days, at this point. In spite of that, my shiny, heroic side saw the light. No matter how much the old me and the new me duked it out over her, this woman would always have the final say. Because I truly did love her—her outer flamboyance and her inner dedication— and love meant thinking of her first.

"After you," I said. And I meant it.

She responded with a smile, took the ladder's sides, and climbed up before me. As I watched her go, I vowed that from now on there would be a worthy role for a girl in my novels, not just some dame.

Once over the railing and in her sanctuary of delight, she settled me into the softest chair I had ever sat in. It was a pillowy cushion on four stubby legs. I felt more like a baby than I did a man as I snuggled in.

"Wait right there. I will have you feeling better in no

time." She disappeared to another section of her colorful maze where she made kitchen types of noises which filled the air with an exotic aroma. "Breathe this." She suddenly appeared in front of me, her shirt flittering in the breeze. She handed me a steaming cup of something I took a deep breath of and let out a sigh. I never sighed.

"What is it?" I whispered in an unnatural tone.

"My secret concoction. Now, close your eyes and let this warm cloth soothe them." She tipped my head back and placed something balmy and woodsy-scented across my eyes. "Breathe the steam from this cup and rest. When you get up, you will be absolutely refreshed. From now on, we will tend to my wedding and your writing, both. In the meantime, you sit here and recover, and I will work on my wedding dress."

I felt like royalty and had to ask myself again what sort of idiot Dwayne was to be anywhere other than here. She hummed a melodic tune I had never heard before as I drifted away in her tender care and aromatic sensations.

"What do you think?" a feminine voice called. I followed its sound from a deep sleep of wind, water, and colorful sails. I opened my eyes to fabric billowing from a shapely mast as I cast a small boat from the peninsula onto Shale Lake. The fabric twirled with Chastity as she spun in front of me. "Will Dwayne want to marry me in this? I just finished it."

The misty dream dissipated as floor-length lavender with swirls of white and faint green swam with her lithe spinning, the steady breeze through her home adding to the beauty.

"I would," I said before I censored myself. "I mean, Dwayne would be a fool not to... No, that's not what I meant either."

"You mean this dress will do." She beamed. She looked so tiny in the scoop-necked design fitted just below her...I looked elsewhere.

"It will." It would more than do.

She must have removed whatever liquid I had fallen asleep breathing, as well as the eye compress. Free to move, I wallowed myself from the pillowy chair and stood. This girl, no matter how I felt about her, was marrying another man. Not to mention, carrying his child. I rubbed my eyes and focused anywhere except on her. I could do this. I would. For her.

"So, we have today, tomorrow, and the next day to prepare." Chastity bounced eagerly on her toes. The realization we had an extra day made me want to do the same. "Yesterday when I said we had three days, I was counting whole days. That means, officially, we begin today. And since you are a writer, would you create the invitations? Say something fun and romantic. Then we will work on your stories."

"You recall, my specialty is death and destruction." At least it was before I met her.

"Of course. But this is my story, and I don't want anyone killed." She laughed. "Write about love."

Love. I gulped. Writing love into Dwayne's life felt like writing an epitaph for mine. But as she stood there and grinned, words my grandfather would be proud of churned upward from somewhere deep inside and poured from my mouth.

"A vacuum will surround Shale Lake's peninsula on June 20th. On that afternoon, as happened at Creation, love will take pieces of Chastity and Dwayne and unite them in an explosion of life. Anyone nearby will be transformed by the fallout, the twinkling sensation of

stars, sunlight, and water, as they commit their love forever."

Chastity gasped. Her already wide eyes grew wider. "That's beautiful."

"I had to stick in an explosion and some fallout," I muttered, shocked at what must have come from my heart. My publisher would dump me. Even after Seth murdered me.

"Incredible," Chastity more breathed than said. "I knew you could do it, Jim. Quick, write those exact words on this card. And in your best penmanship. We will make twenty and send them out."

Stupidly, I took the card. I didn't create those words, they were in me. Because of her? Or because of something romantically philosophical I had inherited from my grandfather? Like his essence?

"Here are nine more cards. I will do the other ten." She handed them to me. "Are you up for it?"

That and more, but I should tell her no. "I think so."

"Good. While you write yours, I will change. Together we will make the invitations. Later today we will deliver the ones to people who live close and will come. Which means…"

…as they commit their love forever… I looked up, my words still with me, my plan to keep a respectable distance vaporizing into a mist. "Means what?"

"We must take one to my parents." She nibbled her lower lip. My noble intentions teetered more as I focused on her mouth instead of what Seth charged me to focus on.

"You will be fine, Chastity. Wear something loose. They will never know." Even my surreptitious glances hadn't been able to penetrate her flimsy fabric enough to spot any rises and falls in her flesh. "Dang it." I needed to get a grip on myself.

"Dang it? You think Mom and Dad really will know?" She pinched her lips together and placed one hand on her midsection. A support for her and a painful reminder to me that she truly belonged to that other guy.

"No, of course I don't think that. I was chiding myself for forgetting to put gas in my car," I lied.

She frowned. "Oh. I don't know a thing about that. I've never owned a car. Dwayne does, but he takes care of those things. Thank you, though, Jim, for assuring me it will go well with my parents. I can never repay you for all the good you do for me." With a warm smile, she slipped behind one of her fabric walls while I tried not to gouge the invitation with my pen.

"A   vacuum   will   surround   Shale   Lake's peninsula..."

She returned in something so baggy I thought it might be a bedsheet she'd wrapped herself in. "Um, that should do. No one will suspect a thing."

"My parents are used to my styles." She dismissed my surprised look. "Now let's get this done."

The words flowed. Ones so foreign to me my hand faltered, my grandfather's voice rising with mine in my prose. "You're right again," I muttered as if he could hear me.

"Me? I'm right?" She looked up, her cheeks rosy, maybe flushed over the nuptials my words heralded.

"Just talking to myself." My cheeks felt as red as hers looked. As she puzzled over my awkward silence, it dawned on me that if anyone on earth could understand my grandfather, Chastity would. She had proven that when I mentioned him before. "When I was a boy..."

"Someone impacted you greatly." Her eyes glistened, the blue coming alive. "Your grandfather, who you mentioned before, maybe…" She tilted her blonde curls this way and then that. "Because no girlfriend or friend could achieve the trust you have in him. Maybe you didn't fully appreciate the things he said, not the way you do now." She tapped her lips pensively. I envied that finger. Her mouth was the sort an artist would draw. "Yep, it's your grandfather. Not a teacher. Not even a Sunday School teacher. I don't particularly detect God in your reasoning."

"What? How can you say that? Unless you think I've offended Him with my novels…" Something I had never given a thought to until this moment.

"You haven't offended Him. If anything, you think He has offended you."

No one had ever suggested I had it in for God before. "You said I was an answer to your prayer."

"Oh, you are." She came toward me and took my hands. "The perfect answer."

Had Dwayne been an answer to her prayer also? A more intimate prayer for someone who fit her heart? And God chose him instead of me? Maybe because I really did have it in for Him.

I chewed my inner cheek. If this was a story, I would write Dwayne as a nasty trick the devil played on her.

"So," she said, not releasing her hold on my hands. "Tell me more about the grandfather who impacted you so much."

I felt him in the room. Or maybe it was in Grove. Mountain Grove. Or because we had been on his beloved peninsula, she with her yellowish hair. It was as if he joined Chastity and me, and she sensed it too. His hands and heart were in this decrepit building with us, his presence and hers making it feel like a castle instead.

"If it wasn't for him, who knows where you might be now instead of here helping me." She squeezed my hand.

How did she know? Because of Grandpa I came to Grove and searched for a peninsula that brought me to Chastity…who then brought me to it. Even though Seth believed my main purpose here was to meet an informant who dared to malign one of Hitler's men. I let go of her hand. "My grandfather is a wonderful man… But before we discuss him, there are things you should know about." I had to be honest. "Tasks you can't help me with." Like crime and violence, dangerous interviews, and the way I felt about her.

A face unlike any I had ever seen…and never would again…should send my heroic heart to the ladder where I would gather a million splinters in my hands by sliding to the ground, risking pain and infection to keep her safe.

Her features looked watery as I gazed at her. Tears? I never cried. Her pastel throw rugs turned into colorful puddles blurred by an emotion I had never experienced before.

"You are supposed to be here, Jim. And I am supposed to help you."

For a moment, something ominous crept into my thoughts. Something of the old crime writer in me, who with several clicks of a typewriter's keys could turn any story the direction I wanted. I welcomed him back, then set him aside. Because in the blue of her eyes, I saw something stronger—my promise.

If friendship was defined by a long period of time and a large number of interactions, Chastity didn't qualify. And maybe my initial carnal fascination which became a pitter-patter my heart couldn't beat without didn't meet the definition of love. But she was at least partially right. For three days we were supposed to be together and help each other. For three days we had an eternity.

Chapter 7

A vacuum will surround Shale Lake's peninsula...

The first line I had imagined for Chastity's invitations hovered in my thoughts. "I will help you finish writing these." I tapped the ten cards she had given me. "I can mail the ones that need to be sent, but after that, I have to go." It sounded wrong on the heels of our mutual promises to help each other. And it looked wrong on her face. Time restraints weren't the reason I needed to go. Distance was. I had plenty of time to get to my room and wait for instructions on where to meet Randy Reed. But I wanted an immeasurable distance between Chastity and those I would deal with later tonight.

"You need to go?" She scrunched her face. "But I thought..."

"A prior commitment. It was arranged before I met you...well, 'in the works' might be a better way to phrase it." Somehow that part of my life kept tangling with this one. "Nothing I need help with."

"You know I would help you." The earnest look on her face promised she would set her wedding aside to come to my aid. My heart rate kicked up at my importance to a girl I believed would never lie.

A less noble man would have taken advantage of her willing sacrifice and distracted her for three days. Without a wedding, there might be no future with Dwayne.

"No," I snapped, putting an end to the temptation.

"Goodness. You certainly sound like you don't want my help." She looked hurt.

"No, not 'no' to you. Well, yes, 'no' to you, but I meant 'no' to me." I thumped my forehead with the heel of my palm. "Let me begin again."

"Something is bothering you, Jim. I don't know what it is, but if it's me, I will step aside and leave you alone."

Could she do that? Of course, she could. She was about to marry the love of her life. I was just a helper. A bridesmaid, essentially. I weighed my next three days with her against three days without her. How could I ever go back to the humdrum existence of writing novels when I could live one with her? "You don't bother me, Chastity. My publisher gave me an assignment that is a solitary job. An interview. A couple of them in fact. Your presence would be…distracting." For me, Reed, and Clyde. For any man in the area.

"I knew you wrote for the *Times*."

"You did?"

Chastity didn't look well-read, yet she was familiar with everything I did in the literary world. However she came by her knowledge of my talents, she trusted them. And because of that, she trusted me. And I her.

"I know everything there is to know about you, Jim Turner. I told you that." Her easy smile returned. "Answers to prayers are gifts. You don't just look at the package and say thanks. You admire it from every angle, then unwrap it one section at a time. When the final layer is removed and the gift revealed, you lift it out to hold and behold it. Always."

I felt naked in front of those blue eyes, and safe in

those hands. It was like being born into adoring gazes and warm hugs. Better, even. If Dwayne didn't get back soon, he would find himself standing alone on the peninsula. "Chastity…"

She raised a finger. "Don't thank me for that. I thank you, instead. Not everyone is an answer to prayer. Not everyone can be, but you truly are." With lips like no other, she mouthed, "Thank you." Then something else. Something that brought color to her cheeks and more blue to her eyes.

My legs turned molten, or I would have wrapped her in my arms. Kissed her. The heat of my face and speed of my heart must have liquified what used to be solid rock.

On that afternoon, as happened at Creation, love will take pieces of two and unite them in an explosion of life.

It was happening today, in Chastity's home…

"So, if you tell me what time you need to go, I will honor that," she said with conviction. "That's the other thing you do with gifts. You are very careful with them."

The "I do" I was ready to shout…vanished. You didn't become one with a gift or an answer to prayer. That honor belonged to someone much more special.

I faltered. I had misread her. I needed to go. An inner tremor sent fissures through every reason to stay. Go. Stay. Chastity didn't own a clock that I could see, so I glanced at my watch, then at the brightly lit outdoors. Anywhere except at an expression which must not be as confused as mine probably looked.

Seth expected me to be in my room well before six, which meant I ought to be there by five. He would want to talk first. Did I care? Not as much as I cared about deciphering what sort of gift I was to Chastity. Surely, in her flowery world, there would be a daisy…*she loves me, she loves me not…*

"After all, we have tomorrow and the next day." She tried to bolster me, bolster both of us.

Four o'clock would be plenty good for Seth. Three, in case someone was watching me closely today. No, two o'clock to be safe.

"I need to leave at six o'clock or shortly after." I berated myself for my weakness. "No, that's not right. I should be back at the hotel by five thirty. Make that one o'clock." What was I thinking? I should be nowhere near her today of all days, but I couldn't leave. "That doesn't give us much time."

"You are a bigger help than you will ever know, Jim Allan Turner." The way she said my full name made writing wedding invitations far more important than any article for the *Times*. But the way she looked told me I should write them and then go. Little pieces that felt Dwayne's absence shone deep within her gaze. Frightened niches of "what-if" that no amount of planning could ease. I saw her inner worry that he wouldn't come. That he might no longer want her. Or their child. Chastity could handle being alone, but she couldn't handle being without Dwayne.

The vacuum that would surround Shale Lake's peninsula the day they married now welled up inside of me. An isolating aloneness came with it. The object of my affection longed for another.

Anyone nearby will be transformed by the fallout…

That would be me.

…the twinkling sensation of stars, sunlight, and water, as they commit their love forever.

The short distance I had climbed up my mountain gave me a perspective I didn't want to face. From where I stood, I could see that a broken heart beat with twice the fervor a whole one did. And that the two parts would forever wish they could become one. With a special someone, with Chastity especially, but they never would. Because love always did what was best for the one they beat for.

Chapter 8

"Where have you been?" Seth barked into the phone.

I glanced around the hotel lobby wondering if anyone else could hear him. No one was nearby except Kevin, the morning desk clerk, who wore the same scowl he had when he handed me a stack of urgent messages from Seth moments ago.

I needed a response which would protect my ear as well as my heart. Seth wouldn't want to hear how painful writing ten invitations to Chastity's wedding had been. Or how unnerving it was to learn that the thirteen invited people who wouldn't come were names and addresses Dwayne had given her. While she rallied with an "any friend of Dwayne's is a friend of mine," I wondered what sort of man would ruin his fiancée's big day by sending announcements to thirteen addresses, none of which were in Illinois? The old Jim Turner in me planned to find out, while the new Jim grieved at writing Chastity out of my life.

"You were supposed to stick close to your room today," Seth thundered. He would reach through the phone and choke me if I told him I'd spent my afternoon prolonging the agony of putting an end to my ecstasy with Chastity by penning each invitation at a snail's pace. "I have been calling since early this morning, and according to the clerk there, you've been nowhere around."

"I was busy." Busy staring at my painfully written invitations to the ceremony for which Chastity had then begun to rehearse her vows. But thankfully stopped. I left at that point. And chose to do the only heroic thing I could—drop off the invitations to Dwayne's guests at the post office. After I made a list of their names and addresses. "I'm here now."

Low voices behind me caught my attention. I glanced over my shoulder. Wally stood at the counter where Kevin had been. We locked gazes. Should I ask him if he knew anything about the woman from the night before? The sound of rustling paper drew my attention from Wally to a man in one of the lobby chairs, his head and shoulders hidden behind a newspaper. Was he the one who had done this very same thing yesterday evening? From the chest down, he looked the same.

"Are you sure the *Times* sent that woman to watch me?" I queried Seth in a whisper.

"What woman?"

"Last night. The woman who told me I was being watched."

"Forget about her. All you need to know is that the paper is keeping an eye on you."

Wally was, as well. His hands looked busy, but his eyes followed me. The man reading the newspaper hadn't budged. I shoved the stack of Seth's demands to call him into my pocket. Was Chastity the only person in Grove I could trust?

"Listen to me." Seth broke into my tumbling thoughts. "Randy Reed confirmed with my contact at the *Times* that he will meet you tonight. He feels safer under the cover of darkness. Can't blame him for being scared.

In fact, if the paper wasn't paying him abundantly, I doubt we would have heard from him again."

Strangely, I found Reed's horrifying reality calming. Threats of death called to the writer in me. The old Jim, the one Chastity chose to help her. "Where is Reed?"

"How do I know? No one will give me any details. That's why you need to be in your room. Stay there until you are contacted." Seth's voice rose in pitch. He sounded angry and afraid at the same time.

"Got it," I said. "Headed there now. Talk to you later." I hung up before Seth could rant more. I didn't need his panic on top of my own turbulence. I set the receiver on its handset and turned. The man with the newspaper was disappearing around a corner, leaving me with a fleeting glimpse of his profile before he vanished.

"Sir…" Wally said, as if we were co-conspirators. We weren't.

I gave him a wave and darted to my room. After bolting the door behind me, I walked to my dresser and studied my reflection in its mirror. Remnants of Chastity still clung to me. Not just the effects of her fruity aroma and pastel world, but the sorrow that knowing her had left in my eyes. The same pain I had spotted in hers—the awareness that you couldn't live without the one person who meant the world to you. In my case, I had to. She didn't. Thankfully, though, she hadn't said that or even mentioned his name.

"Say goodbye to her. To everything about her," I admonished my pitiful reflection. Every bit of Chastity had to go. Any remnant would distract me from an interview Reed might well refuse to give if he got a whiff of her lemony scent or spotted my frailty.

I stripped, scrubbed thoroughly in a tub of water, then dressed in fresh clothing at lightning speed. Chastity-free on the outside, I waited, sitting on the foot of my bed in a silent room, staring at a typewriter I would use again. Because Grandpa's gold pen would remain untouched by yet another Turner who loved and lost.

By the time the knock came, my typewriter was barely visible in the darkened room. I jumped at the sudden sound, then berated myself as I cracked the door to a man who snapped an order to come with him. I refused. Car keys jangling where he could see them, I said I would follow him instead. Seth would kill me if my standoff cost the *Times* this interview. Better to be murdered by him, though, than the tank of a woman the paper supposedly sent. Or by this substantial man. Would Chastity wonder where I had gone? What had happened? I had promised I would return to help her tomorrow. Worst of all, if after three days she still hadn't heard from me, would she even care?

The man grunted. I shook off Chastity's presence, locked my door, and hurried after his fast-moving figure. His dark clothing blended with the night as everything of Chastity vanished. Her colorful world, her light breezes, her blue eyes…all of it was left behind as I hopped into my car and followed him to wherever Randy Reed waited.

****

"I'm Jim Turner," I said to the eye peering from a barely opened motel room door I had been told to knock on. A seedy place far from the much nicer one Seth…the *Times*…had chosen for me. "I'm here to…"

"Shhh," came a hiss from the inside as the eye roved from the right to the left, scouring the parking lot behind me. I couldn't help myself and glanced over my shoulder. Whoever had led me here had driven away and was nowhere to be seen. "Show me some ID," a husky voice whispered from behind the door.

I fumbled for my wallet, the only thing I was allowed to bring besides a pen and some paper—no satchel and no jacket, per Reed's paranoia. Once I had the wallet opened, I held it close to the door. A man's hand shot out and took it.

"Hey…"

"Shush," he snapped. The eye reappeared and looked me up and down. "You fit the description I was given. Come in."

The door opened enough for me to slither into a room that reeked with the stagnant fumes of body odor and cigarette smoke. I batted my eyes in the dark when the door was shut and bolted behind me. A shiver of panic crept up my back, and my throat refused to swallow.

"Can you see okay?" a husky whisper asked as rough hands patted my trouser pockets and legs. Looking for a weapon, no doubt. One I wished I had.

"Not really." I fumbled away from the man who had to be Reed, my arm sweeping empty air so I wouldn't trip over a chair. Dang it. I needed to see his face, how he held himself, in order to discern whether his story was truth or bluff. "Hard to write when it's this dark."

"Anyone follow you?"

The fact that I was more equipped to write this stuff than live it sent another chill up my spine. "I didn't see anyone."

"That doesn't mean a thing. And there were two of you. Two cars when you pulled in. Only supposed to be one." His footsteps shuffled around me.

"Someone came to my door for me, but I refused to ride with him and followed in my own car instead. I don't know who he was or where he went." I felt like an idiot. Once again, if this happened in my books, the hero would die. I wanted to check my shirt for any remnant of Chastity's lemony scent. Something was causing me to act like a moron with my head in the clouds.

"I expected better from you, but I guess you're just a reporter."

"I write books too."

He snorted in the darkness. I heard shuffling again and the scrape of a chair. Eventually a tiny glow lit the far corner of the room following the click of a switch. A dark figure stood beside a small table with a lamp shrouded by fabric draped over it. "Sit here." It sounded like he kicked a chair. "Don't remove the cloth from the lamp. You should have enough light to write by."

He moved into the dark as I made my way to the table and chair. "Thanks," I said, wondering where he was while rebuking myself for spending more time pondering Chastity than I did this guy and his self-inflicted danger. Once settled into the chair, I extracted paper and pen from my pocket, then wrote the time, date, and subject at the top of a clean page.

"What you writing?" Reed's voice barked from the opposite corner along the same back wall where I sat, neither of us near the front window or door.

"Just details for my own records."

"No names, no descriptions, no nothing that points to me."

It was too dark to see him anyway, and I had no idea what his real name was. "Absolutely."

He didn't offer me anything to eat or drink, though a glass of water would have been wonderful on my dry throat. I tried not to tap my pen as we sat in silence. When he finally began, his voice came lower and sounded even huskier. I had to strain to distinguish his words, but his fear was crystal clear. I could smell his sweat from across the room.

As I took notes, even though I couldn't see him, experience at writing crime told me his details weren't rehearsed or memorized, and therefore likely to be true. When he explained how he came to learn about Hitler's deserter and his lover, I believed him.

"I actually flirted with her," Reed confessed. "She was new in my area of Chicago, a real beauty I spotted going in and out of the synagogue. I rent a room above a mom-and-pop shop across the street from it. I see everything."

I caught the slight hindsight of daring pride. Here was a nobody who had broached Hitler's realm, drawn by a forbidden beauty. I wrote furiously, capturing every word while adding my interpretation of his feelings. This was a pencil-chewing tale, but I kept writing, jotting two words for every one of his, the horror of his situation filling my page.

"She didn't flirt back, thank God. Never even spoke to me. Now I know why. Of course, she might not have been able to speak English, for all I know." Reed paused. "He spoke English, though, good English, with a heavy German accent. But that's not what clued me in. It was the way he stood and what I saw in his eyes. He was trained, a regimented man who could kill for a cause. Except for…"

My hand trembled as I waited for him to continue;

my heart hammered, loud enough he likely heard it.

"…except for something soft in that cold gaze. It was in both of them. He had wreaked terror, and she had been terrorized…but neither did it to the other. What I saw had to be love."

Suddenly the dark, smelly room filled with light breezes, soft colors, the lemony scent of Chastity, another forbidden and taboo beauty. Meeting her convinced me a person could love someone they knew for less than a day. Was that what had happened to these two while still overseas? In the minutes allotted to Hitler's soldier to scope out a neighborhood before taking everyone captive, did love happen? Turning his world upside down as mine had been? A soldier, trained to be heartless, found his heart beating at their brief encounter. And he seized the opportunity to save her life while risking his own.

"Do you know how they met?" My voice wavered and I cleared my throat. "How did they have a chance to know they loved each other?" They surely didn't have three days. Three minutes was more likely all the time the soldier had before he knew. I gripped my pen in a chokehold.

"You gotta understand how I figured the whole situation out in order to put together how they met. First, he never came near the synagogue. I found out about him by following her. Like I said, she was a real looker, so a guy does things. You know, things he normally wouldn't do. Anyway, I tailed her quite a ways. Once I saw who she met, I suspected right away what he might be. After some digging around, I pieced together who and what he was, and then things he'd done or at least been a part of."

"How?" I blurted, shocked at this man's cunning.

The government put a lid on what could be broadcast, which meant a lock on details very few in the States would know.

"You're the reporter. You tell me how someone gets a story. Sometimes it costs you."

I ignored his sneer and thought better of explaining I wasn't shocked at the means of rooting out information, but at his ability to. Even without being able to see Randy Reed in the dark room, he didn't strike me as a man who maneuvered through life by wit. His sort manipulated it by desperation.

"You trust your sources, then," I prodded him.

"More than you trust me."

I bit back a remark that would have resulted in Reed putting a stop to this interview. "It's the reader who we want to trust you. It's my job to give them enough information to do that. I can write this up as a story or as a plausible report. To do the latter, your sources have to be credible."

He said nothing for a few minutes. "I got connections, none of which I will divulge. But tell your readers what they already know. We all got family, friends, and neighbors over there. People talk when they've been scared or hurt. There are things all of us need to get off our chests. Or get vengeance for. Or, as in the case of those hoping for citizenship or acceptance here, information they hope will improve their chances."

"Good enough." Every American citizen would believe Reed based on that. "What about her?"

"I learned about her the same way I did about him. Family is important when you're Jewish. It's who you are and who you came from. They are tight. They are faithful. There is no such thing as a distant relative to them, even if that family member lives overseas. I know all this because I've lived in that neighborhood long enough they're comfortable with me. I see and hear things, making it easy to find out her family name. Which she kept, by the way. And why not, when many of them have the same name? Anyway, I noticed she was accepted into the synagogue community with relish, which I figured had something to do with her looks, but also a possible story. After seeing her meet up with him, I nosed around and learned her parents and their daughter…probably her…had been reported among the dead." Reed paused. He drew a long breath. "You don't have to be a genius to realize her path crossed that soldier's in a fateful way. 'Fortuitous' might be a better word, because look at what he did for her. Maybe for her parents too, but I don't know for sure. I imagine he was doing his job and got caught short when he saw her. Love at first sight, if you believe in that sort of thing." In the dark I felt Reed shrug. Maybe a dismissal of love, but more likely a dismissal of the girl who got away. Fortunately for him.

I thumped my pen on the paper. "So she's likely been declared dead officially. But what about him?"

"Will be dead, when he's found. I thought at first he might still be active under Hitler and hiding the true reason for his visits here by pretending to root out those who escaped to this country. To buy him some time, you know. Cover his tracks while he secures the two of them here with new identities. But I know better now. Being a deserter, he might have done a good job of hiding her, but unless he did a superb job of faking his own death over there, Hitler will be looking for him."

"Are you concerned that you are increasing their

chances of being discovered by coming out with this story?" I found myself siding with the two lovers. The woman was alive and safe. She might have fallen for the wrong man, but he clearly loved her, by my grandfather's definition of a hero. Whereas Randy Reed...

"This is the opportunity of a lifetime and the scoop of the century," Reed snapped. "Are you saying you don't want to be the one who does what Hitler failed to do? Keep track of his own? And do something about it?"

I wasn't sure if it was terror or fury that set every arm hair on end. "Listen to me. You are a part of their story now. You've inserted yourself into it. All I am asking is 'Why?' How do you feel about that? Every reader will want to know."

"I feel justified. I'm saving her in a far better way than that soldier did. Don't you see that? She will be better off when this guy is rooted out and destroyed. I'm not the bad guy—that soldier is. She will be safe. Completely free. Every synagogue in the country will protect her, and so will I."

I laid my pen down. I couldn't write. Instead of Reed, I heard myself. I was no better than he was, the way I disregarded Dwayne and undermined his commitment to Chastity. Chances were good that, like the two of them, Hitler's soldier was this Jewish woman's answer to her prayers. Not Randy Reed. And not me.

If I loathed this sweaty informant hiding in the dark, I had to loathe myself. "I think we're done here."

"Hardly," he spouted. "I put my life on the line for this. I'm doing a good deed, and if you think you're going to waltz out of here with half the story, you're wrong. You won't go nowhere."

I assumed Reed to be twice my size, and he was also desperate. I considered my chances of escape as he dragged a chair to the door and planted himself in front of it with a thunk. "You are easy to find," he warned me. "We will finish this, you will write it, and we will both survive. She will too. Got it?"

He probably heard me swallow. "All right." I got it, but I wondered how many of us would really survive after exposing a beautiful woman who was "taboo" for one of Hitler's men.

"Good. Now I will tell you what else I know about the guy so he can be found. Not his name, though I uncovered it. That trail to me would be too easy to trace."

I grimaced at such cowardice, knowing he couldn't see it. I also seethed at being trapped with two men who cloaked selfish and despicable acts under the guise of something noble. Myself as well as Reed.

My ire remained, but my terror increased as he resumed his tale, and my words began to draw this soldier…a heartless tool brought to life by love.

"Not that many in this country would pay attention to him," Reed explained. "Since he has to be sharp enough to outwit a man trying to rule the world, it shouldn't take him long to figure out who could give him away. And because I will never show my face in that area again, she might notice that I, the man who flirted with her, is missing. Creating another way her soldier could guess I'm the informant."

I almost admired Reed's cunning. He would need it, since he chose to match wits with men who terrorized a large portion of the world. At least the man I came close to offending was an ordinary fellow named Dwayne.

"Don't write this down," Reed commanded. I laid my pen aside and listened as he drew a general verbal picture of this soldier. He allowed me to write the guy's heart, even parts of his heinous history Reed got from a loose-lipped prisoner hoping for something in exchange, but only a little about the soldier's face or stature. By the time Reed finished, I had gleaned a perfect image of Hitler's deserter in my mind—his above average height, his solid build, his set jaw, hazel eyes, and light-colored hair. I even knew he had a watchful eye without letting it be noticed, and that the veins protruded on the backs of his hands when he spoke.

"And her?" I asked, to which I received a glowing description of the deserter's perfect complement. Beautiful, attractive in form and style, and safely kept in the soldier's shadow.

"I have a theory," Reed said after a long pause. "And you can write this down if you want, because I'm pretty sure I'm right. This guy is building a life here in the States. Somewhere safe where they can both hide. But instead of doing it directly, he is taking a wide sweep. You know, a dozen directions, fake trails to fake names and places, a course spread so thin no one will be able to follow it."

My heartrate kicked up as I wrote that down. Something Reed said bothered me. "So he might be spreading his time out between her and thirteen other names and places, plus the one place he intends for them to live with new identities."

"You got it. Except, I didn't say thirteen, but it could be. It could be twenty."

"I had no reason for saying thirteen." A chill trickled over my skin. "The point you're making is that he could be anywhere."

"And be anybody," Reed added. "Except to me. I would recognize him in a heartbeat."

As much as I hated to admit it, Reed was right. The guy had to be very creative to go somewhere and be someone else. So he could ultimately be with the one he loved enough to risk his life for. I flipped my pen back and forth between two fingers. "Anything else?"

"Yeah, before you send this to the *Times*, I want to see what you wrote."

"We can meet here again." I stuffed my pen back into my pocket and folded my notes, hoping Reed couldn't see the tremor in my hands.

"No. I will find you. Like I said, you're easy to find."

The chill returned. Seth had better make sure I was well paid for this interview. I rose from my chair, but no sound came from near the door. Reed hadn't moved.

"Have it ready by tomorrow." Then he stood. I eased toward the sliver of streetlight where he cracked open the door.

I paused before I left the motel room. "One more question. Is this deserter tall, or extra tall?" The sort of height that required a custom-made bicycle seat. The sort of person who would create thirteen fake identities to send invitations to.

Reed paused. A nauseating mixture of sweat and stale cigarette breath nearly choked me. "I said tall. Meaning average tall. He won't stand out in a crowd, so don't think you can peg him. Only I can do that."

I wanted to thank him and run to my car at the same time. Not thank him for the interview but for the fact Hitler's deserter couldn't possibly be Dwayne. Or

Chastity be a part of the deserter's wide and cunning sweep to hide behind.

As Reed closed and locked his door behind me, I forced myself to maintain a reasonable pace to my car but scoured my surroundings as I went. Once inside the vehicle, I wasted no time locking all four doors. I wanted to grab the steering wheel and drag in deep breaths of relief, but I sat motionless. A man in Reed's position would be watching from his window. Someone else could…would…be watching as well, according to the stocky woman. I fumbled and missed the ignition twice before I finally inserted the key and started the car.

Reed would find me tomorrow, which meant I would write the interview tonight. But I wouldn't send it to Seth or the *Times* yet, even after Reed approved it. Randy Reed would balk at that as well, but I would claim it was for research. Good journalists checked their facts. I would stall him, Seth, and the *Times* for three days. They would be demanding a story I wouldn't give them until I kept my promise to Chastity. She would have her wedding. I would keep her safe from anyone watching me or tailing Reed until then by keeping them at bay. After that, her life and mine would part. And Grandpa's peninsula would be the memory of a distant fantasy in my mind, just like it was in his.

Chapter 9

I have a story.

I didn't have a story, but I had an article to write. Morning light softened the rectangle of closed curtains on my room's window. I hadn't typed a single word, nor had I slept much, most of my night wasted wearing a path between my typewriter and Grandpa's gold pen.

Reed would find me at some point today and demand to read what I had written. I gazed at the blank sheet of paper curled around the typewriter's cylinder, ready to go. I could stall him with the excuse I didn't recognize him and therefore wouldn't release the article to him. After all, I had nothing to go on other than his voice and the smell of cigarettes and fear.

My typewriter waited like an old friend in the morning light. Jim Turner from New York could hammer out a gripping retelling of Reed's account…if the Jim Turner in his grandfather's Mountain Grove could get past the beating of Hitler's ex-soldier's heart. Looking for inspiration in my notes and Reed's vengeful motives had failed me, the deserter's passion softening the edges of his crime, giving it new angles and reasons to justify right in his wrongs.

I have a story.

I picked up my pace back and forth across the room. Grandpa had a story. So did Reed. One was still obscure and called for the gold pen, while the other was openly blunt and suitable for my typewriter. I marched to the window and threw the curtains aside. Even the small brown-haired woman I'd met my first day in Grove had a story. In fact, *I have a story* was her exact claim. After which I saw Chastity…

"It's a love story, not a war crime." Seth's worst nightmare dawned brighter than the rising sun.

Look for the relationship when you write, son. There always is one, whether it is between a man and a woman, a boy and his dog, a sailor and his ship, or a country and its enemy. The most daring conquests involve the heart. There is no battle, no story, until there is heart.

With my increased inner illumination, I felt my grandfather's smile. And envisioned his satisfied nod that I finally saw what he had seen for ages.

"I have a story," I said to my tired reflection when I moved to the dresser's mirror. My eyes brightened. I truly did have a story, and it was a love story. The weariness on my face vanished. Words erupted from a fount deep within. Not the sort I had written for years, which detailed a criminal's master plan and some detective's cunning ability to foil it. These words had color. They spoke of life and death but couched them in love. There was a time to kill and a time to build. Somehow the two were entwined.

Grandpa's gold pen glittered in the background of my reflection. Increasing daylight highlighted it on the nightstand near the bed.

Type all the stories you want, son, but when you're ready to put life on a page, use this.

I eyed the family heirloom I had assumed I would pass on unused like every other Turner had.

Someday, son, something will send your moral

compass into a tailspin. Gravity will vanish, and you will fling your guards aside. What has always been singular vision will suddenly become kaleidoscopic. When that happens, grab this pen and write. With blood as your ink, write your heart on the page.

Everything I was experiencing in Grove was Grandpa's "someday" as well. My moral compass spun erratically because I pined for another man's fiancée. Gravity had no power over me as I scaled my inner mountain. And guards I had put up were more likely to get me killed than to protect me. No longer did I see a simple plot of good versus evil. Because from now on, murder could be romantic and dying an act of saving love.

I retrieved Grandpa's pen from the nightstand, the gold warm in my fingers. I had a story, this pen had a story, and so did everyone involved in my trip to Grove. Each one of us had a mountain and a love story to tell as we scaled it.

Racing to my desk, I scooted my typewriter to the side and sat down to fill the pen with ink, possibly for the first time in its existence. The moment its tip touched a clean sheet of paper, a lemony scent filled the room. The essence of passion for a woman bled onto the page as Grandpa's heart appeared. So did the heart of Hitler's deserter, the three of us giving up everything because we were willing to end up with nothing for the sake of someone we loved. Grandpa had certainly left someone precious behind. Hitler's ex-soldier gave up everything about his own life for the woman he saved, and maybe would ultimately give her up. Surely that was what my grandfather did. He must have walked away from the one who meant the world to him, because it was best for her.

The same price I would pay for Chastity. My hand moved. Ink flowed. I ripped out my heart and each of theirs and wrote three full pages of the most incredible stories ever told.

I had never written like this. Nor had I ever soaked my shirt in the process, sweating more than Reed had the night before. He perspired fear, whereas I drenched my clothing with ardor. The gold pen brought honesty to the page in the form of naked truth. Things not everyone should see.

I slid the typewriter in front of me and set the handwritten pages to the side. My room filled with the familiar clacking of keys as my fingers gleaned an article fit for the *Times* from the heart Grandpa's pen had poured into the stories stacked close by.

Reed wanted to portray himself as a hero who undid international enemies, but in the story I had penned, another champion had emerged. One I had to keep fairly invisible in the article because I chose to keep the deserter safe. Reed would be furious if he saw the truth of what he had done. His goal to help the Jewish woman brought out the real story. A love story between two enemies. Romeo and Juliet. Right wedded to wrong. I put Reed's efforts to free her from the soldier into the article, something that would only bind the two lovers tighter. In my written story, I gave much credence to the enemy Reed had made human by giving him a heart. But in the article, I said just enough for Hitler's ex-soldier to decide how to best use that heart—to create a future for her which either included or excluded him based on what was best for her. Because I assumed he would read it.

My fingers slowed and my chest felt heavy as I concluded an article in which I could see a story that included mine and Grandpa's along with that of the two lovers. I ended the article with Reed's statement of how he had found his proof, then typed my name, though the *Times* said they wouldn't reveal my identity or Reed's.

Someone knocked on my door as I removed the final page from the typewriter.

"If that's you, Reed, the article is finished. You're just in time," I shouted.

"I don't know who Reed is, sir. This is Kevin, the desk clerk. You have a message."

"If it's from Seth, tell him I'm busy and to stop interrupting me," I shouted again.

"Sir, it isn't from Seth. It's your grandfather. He..."

I flew to the door and opened it so fast, Kevin's hair lifted in the draft. His eyes widened as the sprigs across his forehead dropped back into place.

"My grandfather?" Shouting was no longer called for, but my voice still boomed.

Kevin cautiously extended a note to me. "He said it's not urgent. You needn't call him back."

I whipped Grandpa's folded message from Kevin's hand, then inwardly chastised myself. Apparently good manners went out the window with my guards. "Thank you," I managed twice, as I closed the door.

"You're welcome, sir." Kevin spoke from the other side.

Remorseful, I opened the door again. "I'm sorry for my rudeness. Truly. A lot has happened, and I haven't slept a wink..."

"Wally told me as much. Normally I don't pay any attention to him, but by the looks of you..."

"Wally said that? How would he know?"

Kevin's face darkened in color. "He's different...

He scares me, actually."

I scoured the area behind Kevin. Had the solid woman meant Wally was watching me? The avid fan of my books? My whole body went cold. He didn't recite my list of characters alphabetically because he treasured them. He did it because he wasn't familiar with them and had memorized their names in order. "What time does Wally come to work?"

"He won't be in today. He is taking the night off."

Next time I wrote a book on crime, I would have the bad guy fall head over heels for some babe…woman…and become disoriented enough to turn into an easy target. Like I had. Except I wasn't a bad guy. "You probably have no idea where Wally lives…"

Kevin's vigorous head shake dashed any hope. "No, sir. We aren't friends."

"There must be an employee file somewhere."

"In Chicago, I imagine. The hotel's owner lives and works there. We rarely see him."

Wally, like Hitler's deserter, could be anywhere. I shuddered. "Thank you, Kevin."

He backed away as I closed my door. My room felt colder than it had earlier, the euphoria from writing with the gold pen diminished. Could Wally be tied to Reed's story? And therefore tied to me as its writer? I shook my head. That was a little too fantastic to believe since no one knew I came to Grove with the interview on my list except Seth and the *Times*…and Reed. And possibly anyone spying on him. I began to pace. Neither did anyone know Jim Turner the author came to town to find his grandfather's peninsula, but Chastity had recognized me instantly. And had taken me to the very lake where it lay.

I swiped perspiration from my brow. Romeo never doubted Juliet. Hitler's soldier must have doubted everyone he met in this country as well as in his own…except for her. The woman he loved.

I gazed at Grandpa's folded note, my mind whirling with images of Wally, Chastity, and Reed. Grandpa said it wasn't urgent, but my questions regarding the other three could be a matter of life or death. And in one case, a matter of love or…not. Which felt worse than death.

I slid Grandpa's note into my pocket and bolted from my room and jumped into my car. With a roar unsuitable for an idolized writer in a town this size, I shot from the hotel parking lot and headed to the one place where words turned into warm feelings, not criminal plots where those we loved became villains. Grandpa's peninsula would right all wrongs and clarify the uncertain, even if it became the place where he and I said goodbye to the ones we loved.

The sparkles on Shale Lake grew brighter as I stepped to the peninsula's tip. It seemed to recognize and welcome me. "You remember my grandfather," I corrected its frolicking waves. Sparkles? Frolicking?

I dropped cross-legged onto the ground and stared across the shimmering… Shimmering? My words truly were turning into warm feelings. Seth was right to worry about what a trip here would do to me, and more right to insist upon a meeting between me and a heinous ex-con to preserve my edge.

Shutting my eyes, I lay back on the sandy shore. The water still shimmered, but in my ears where teeny sensations of watery applause filled the air. I wanted to drown in the sound, sail on the breeze, and live under a sky the same color as Chastity's eyes—forever. Eyes that would never betray me…or anyone.

Including Dwayne.

I lay quietly. My decision shouldn't be whether I could trust her but whether she would be able to trust me to be the hero she needed, to sacrificially love her like Grandpa loved his special someone when he must have chosen to let go for her own good. Like Hitler's ex-soldier would love his intended by marrying her now that he'd given up everything he possessed to save her.

I loved Chastity enough to walk away if it was for her own good. Crawl away, maybe, but I would go. I also loved her enough to leave the old Jim Turner, the author, behind if it was the only way to marry her. If she wanted me…

Did Grandpa know how the woman he for some reason left behind felt about him? Or was he strictly heroic enough to break his own heart and walk away?

I slipped my fingers into my pocket and fished around for his note. What happened to him here? And how did it pertain to me? Unfolding his message with one hand, I shielded my eyes from the sunlight with my other.

You will know, because you already do.

What? What did I know? I did a quick review of my past, my ordinary family…other than Grandpa…who did nothing noteworthy. My own personal background revealed no special knowledge other than a keen ability to create and destroy fictional bad guys.

What else did I know? That three men—Grandpa, the deserter, and I—fell for three impossible-to-obtain women. Grandpa apparently let his go, Hitler's deserter let everything else go. And I…

With blood as your ink, write your heart on the page.

Was I to merely write about it? Because in the other two heroes' cases, their lovers loved them in return? That was the reason I would write from a broken heart. As the third hero, I wouldn't selflessly walk away from or marry the one I loved. I wouldn't even lose her in the end, because I never really had her. I'd be left with only a story. Hadn't Grandpa also said…

Not every ending is a happy one, but if it is the right one, that is all that matters.

A cold horror crept over me. I could continue to write heroes into long lives and criminals into demise because those endings were right and happy and gave readers hope in a world threatened by war. But for myself, could I write an unhappy ending and forfeit the girl I believed I came here to meet? No. Not if she felt for me what I felt for her.

"I'm sorry, Grandpa. If Chastity loves me and wants to be with me, I refuse to lose her. Even if that is what you have been trying to prepare me for, all these years. I will write, though. I will write my heart on the page and rewrite history for every Turner who passed the gold fountain pen on without using it."

I was reasoning with things I could only sense but not see. Yet what I felt seemed more real than the life I had lived before Grove. My conviction to hold onto Chastity, if she felt the same about me, seemed more binding than one of Seth's contracts. I would write it all. I would write what I knew. Which meant I had to discover what I didn't know—*She loves me, or, she loves me not.*

Chapter 10

I remained on the peninsula's shore, staring up at a sky the same blue as Chastity's eyes. The blood I was supposed to write with pushed slowly through my veins, some of it seeping out onto the sand around me. Seth was wrong about romantic stories. They were far more hard-hitting than crime novels. And Grandpa was right. Heroes of the heart had more courage than any muscleman. Wally, Reed, Hitler, the deserter, the solid woman, and even Dwayne terrified me far less than what lay ahead. *She loves me...she loves me not...* I was going to bleed, no matter what.

The unheroic part of me spoke up and insisted I run away. Go back to New York and pretend no such place as Grandpa's peninsula existed, resume my career of writing good-guy-versus-bad-guy stories, or head overseas as a war journalist. Just me and my typewriter, because using blood for ink was too costly and terrifying.

"Go," the dark voice inside me urged. "Stay," my shiny side countered, "Chastity needs you, and you made her a promise."

"She only needs you until she marries Dwayne," my evil side sneered. "You are wasting your time. Get out while you can."

The battle raged. My soul became a war zone. The casualties mounted to greater numbers than in Europe. There was blood everywhere as I lay on this finger of land that jutted into Shale Lake. "Save yourself!" my dark side screeched. "No, you have a story to write," my bright side insisted. "You know that's why your grandfather gave you the gold pen and sent you here. Stay and finish it for him and for you…no matter what!"

"No matter what" meant Chastity might not have feelings for me, and my story might not have a happy ending. But no story at all…I couldn't do that to my grandfather.

The crunch of footsteps silenced the argument between my inner voices. The presence of another person disrupted a solitude I desperately needed. My breathing changed. So did my heart rate. Reed, the last person in the world I wanted to see, was good to his word. Grandpa was right that Reed's story was a love story. Now the snitch wanted to assure himself I had besmirched the couple on the run enough to destroy their chances of a future together.

"You found me," I said, my tone curt. I kept my eyes closed and wished him away.

"I never lost you." A lemony scent filled the air instead of sweat and stale cigarette smoke. Chastity? She joined me on the ground. A lump appeared in my throat as we lay side by side on the peninsula. She said nothing, and I couldn't. Had Grandpa done this very thing with someone years ago? Someone who made yellow his favorite color the way Chastity made it mine?

"You're right, you will never lose me, Chastity," I finally managed. But I would lose her if she willingly said "I do" to Dwayne. I would bleed to death while I watched. "You know that, don't you? No matter what happens, you know you will never lose me?" I held my breath, hoping and praying she would make the same promise to me. That she would declare herself forever belonging to me, the man she really loved.

She took hold of my hand. I needed air. "I do, Jim. Yes, I do."

Chastity's big blue eyes glistened when I looked at her. In a sheen not unlike Shale Lake's surface, I searched for her promise but spotted ripples. Her joy teetered in some sort of turbulence.

My good side was right. This poor girl carried a load I had promised to help her with, not add to. Her "yes" that she knew I was faithful to the end amounted to generosity I didn't deserve. Saying "I do" to Dwayne assured her an eternity. Saying it to me didn't even give her three full days of assistance. "I'm sorry…"

She looked as if I had stabbed her rather than repented. "It's not you. It's me." She strained to swallow, rose awkwardly to a sitting position, and propped herself up on stiff arms extended behind her. "I thought… Never mind what I thought. I'm sorry."

"You have nothing to be sorry for." I scrambled to my feet and offered her my hand. "We have two days…" Two days to plan a wedding, and two days before our parting if I didn't do something to secure her affection.

Chastity glanced away, her gaze flitting in every direction as if she had her own Randy Reed lurking around. "It might be better if… I think I can handle the rest of my wedding plans. And my mother will help." At the mention of her mother, she braced herself on one arm and cupped a protective hand over her middle with the other. She looked miserable and utterly alone.

"I promised to help you deliver the local invitations. And go to your parents' house. I would fly to the moon and back if that's what you needed, Chastity. Just tell me what to do." *Let me give you the best two days a girl could have before...* Before she woke up and married me, the right guy, instead of the wrong one. The image cheered me.

Her eyes watered. "I want you to do what you believe is right."

Chasity wasn't ready for what I thought was right. "I will keep my promise to help you for the next two days." I glanced around us, hoping to spot Reed and be done with him for both of our sakes. "But there are some things I need to take care of."

"Of course. We said we would help each other." She looked like I felt deep inside as she stretched her hand upward and took hold of mine. I gazed at her long, graceful fingers, one of which Dwayne would adorn with his commitment. If I let go of it.

Her fruity scent mingled with the aromas of fresh water, trees, and...me...as I raised her to her feet. I desperately needed to clean up if I was going to woo her successfully. I wasn't wearing the past twelve hours well at all.

My face warmed. "Excuse my condition. I was up all night...I wrote..."

"I have my bicycle. You go to your hotel and freshen up. Write more if you..."

"No. Come with me." It was wrong and right at the same time. Even though I had done everything wrong, things that would have wiped out any character in my books, I wanted her close so I could protect her. And keep her every second I could. Help her realize I was the man for her.

Her beautiful eyes widened. "I don't think..."

Before she could remind me of what was right, I did

what was wrong. "Come on." In a matter of minutes, she and her bicycle were in my car, and I was hurrying us to my hotel.

"This is nice," she said with a slight uneasiness as she gazed around the hotel parking lot and then at the building.

I followed her gaze with mine as I searched every car, nook, and cranny for a stout woman, Wally, someone who might be Reed, or anyone who appeared suspicious. Should I take her to my room? Or would the lobby be safer for her—from me.

"It lacks color," I said to blue eyes that lived in a world of pastel hues. Should I, or shouldn't I?

"Sir?" Someone tapped on my window. I jumped and wheeled from Chastity's gorgeous face to Kevin's, leaning close to the glass. "I saw you pull in. That man is on the phone again." Kevin cast a concerned expression toward the lobby. "He says it's extremely urgent."

Opting not to let Chastity see my brutish side when it came to Seth, I thanked Kevin politely and said I would be right there. He bowed and moved away.

"It's my editor on the phone," I explained to Chastity. "And it's never urgent, no matter what he claims, but do you mind?"

She took my hand and gave it a brief squeeze.

Optimistic at even that minute assurance, I checked the parking lot one more time and hurried us to the hotel lobby.

"No one can find Reed." Seth's voice cracked with an uncharacteristic waver when I said "Hello" as politely as I could in case Chastity could hear me. I glanced to where I had suggested she sit in the lobby chairs. She looked out of place in this nice but artificially austere setting of shades of brown. She smiled at me from the same seat the man with the newspaper had occupied recently. She offered a smile to Kevin as well, who stared at her.

"Reed always checks in with the *Times*, some sort of arrangement they have with him, but they haven't heard a thing. Even I tried a number I was given early on—and got nothing." Seth's chair squealed in the background. "Whoever the paper sent there to keep tabs on him, they lost him. He is nowhere to be found."

I forced my attention back to Seth and hunched around the handset. "That's not good."

"Of course it isn't." Seth was no help when assurance was needed. "I'm getting you out of there. Have you sent the article to me and the *Times* yet?"

"No. Reed insisted he had to approve it first." I glanced out the lobby window hoping to spot a smoking, sweaty hulk waiting for me, one big enough to block a hotel room door the way Reed had the night before. I could hear fingers tapping through the phone line, Seth's tension hammering out an uneasy cadence on his desktop.

"I will have your return ticket changed. Get to the airport right away."

I glanced at Chastity again, her big blue eyes on me. Seth was probably right to get me out of here.

"No," I said into the phone.

"No?" Seth yelped. "What do you mean by that?"

"I have things I need to do here." I removed the handset from my ear while my editor screeched. I let him. For all the annoyance I caused Seth, I knew he cared about me.

"Bad connection?" Chastity frowned at the sounds coming from the phone.

"Something like that." By the time Seth paused to catch his breath, I had made a decision. "If Randy doesn't appear by the end of today, I will send the article to the *Times* because they paid for it. But not to you." I had an uneasy feeling. I cared about Seth as much as he cared about me. Cutting him out of the loop might protect him.

The screeching resumed, the last thing I heard as I lowered the handset into its cradle sounded like, "I'm coming there." Seth wouldn't do that.

I stared at the now-silent phone. I should call him back. But I wouldn't leave Grove. If my fate was to lose Chastity in the end, it wouldn't be because I left her behind.

"Something is wrong, isn't it?" Chastity's lemony scent and her gentle voice drew my attention. She stood close, her brows pinched together above the bridge of her nose.

"It's nothing, really. Some flack about an article I wrote. You can't please everyone." I omitted that the "flack" was sheer terror, and "everyone" could include Hitler. I fumbled for her fingers, knowing I couldn't let her out of my sight now. Apparently neither could Kevin, who watched us closely. "Do you mind coming to my room while I clean up? I promise to…"

"I don't mind at all."

…to behave myself. "I promise to smell better when I'm done."

Without a backward glance at Kevin, I hurried Chastity to my hotel room.

"This is nice," she said about a room that would

likely be ransacked soon, my beloved typewriter trashed, blank paper shredded, and my belongings strewn everywhere. If not by an angry Führer, then certainly by Seth.

"I would call it adequate." I gestured toward the desk chair, but she seated herself on the foot of my bed. I couldn't look at her there. Or think about it. "I will hurry." My voice cracked. She crossed her long legs, and I hurried into the small bathroom where I shut the door between us and ran a tub of cold water my body heat would have boiling in seconds.

No noise came from the other room as I dove into the tub and hastily lathered, then rinsed soap from my skin. "Are you all right?" I called. When she didn't respond, I pressed my ear to the door as I raked a towel over my wet skin. "Chastity?" What would at any other time have been a dream to call to her on my bed felt like a nightmare in the silence. What if Reed…or Wally…maybe Kevin… Knotting the towel around my waist like a skirt, I burst through the bathroom door ready to fight.

She looked up from where she sat in my desk chair, tears in her blue eyes. "Jim…" She held my story—my, Grandpa's, and the soldier's love story I had written with the gold pen—against her heart.

"This is beautiful." She gazed at me. Not at me, but inside of me. "I thought so. I just knew…" She rose to her feet. Lemony scent engulfed me, blonde curls blinded me. Yellow was indeed my favorite color as Chastity pressed close, her willowy form a perfect fit against mine. God sure knew what He was doing when he made this particular woman. As did my grandfather when he encouraged me to find his peninsula.

The words I had written didn't create this passion in Chastity's embrace. It was already there. My story…my heart…merely tapped into hers. A heart I felt beating as she pressed close. Or maybe it was mine. Or both.

I didn't care if the knot holding the towel held or not. I let go of it and returned her embrace with both arms, buried my face in her curls, and inhaled her essence. We stood that way, pressing another eternity into a moment. One I would never let go of…especially if I ever lost her. Which I wouldn't. How could I, when she clearly…

"Jim," she whispered. Her warm breath against my bare chest eased into my thoughts.

"Hm?" Not much of a response for a writer.

"They say you can't love two people at the same time." She sounded wistful. Maybe sad.

I regained my hold on my towel's knot.

"They mean the sort of love you wrote about." Her voice vibrated against my chest. She edged backward. When she looked up at me, more tears filled her eyes. "It's impossible to love two with that sort of passion at the same time."

The small distance between us turned into miles. And miles. Another type of eternity. An empty one she placed between us.

"I will get dressed," I choked. She had made her choice. Her heart belonged to only one—in this case, to the other one. If this was what losing her felt like, dying would indeed be easier.

She dropped onto the foot of the bed and perched on its edge, while I returned to the bathroom and in a blind stupor dragged fresh clothing over cold and mummified skin.

Fractured. The word defined the atmosphere in my

room when I returned to where Chastity sat. I gazed at her teary eyes and watched her bite her lower lip as if there was more she wanted to say but didn't. No matter how anxious Seth was for my safety, I couldn't leave her like this. I would stay for the two days I promised her. But in case this decision cost me dearly, I needed to make sure Grandpa knew something of what had happened to me on his peninsula.

"Do you mind if I type a couple of things before we go?"

"I don't mind. I will sit here and wait." Her voice was as wispy as mine. Our mutual understanding as to the only one she could love was heartbreaking to me and probably awkward for her.

With my back to her, I sat in front of my typewriter. My fingers stuttered over the keys, utterly crippled by what Chastity had said. Typing as if I had never seen a typewriter before, I cranked out two copies of the article I had written for Reed—one for the *Times* and the second one to hide. The original would stay with me in case Reed surfaced. Then, I picked up the gold pen.

Eternity. The beginning and the end in a few well-penned words. How appropriate that they be in this place near and dear to your heart. You of all people will understand what I mean.

I folded the paper and slid it into an envelope, writing my grandfather's name on the outside. It was my just-in-case note to him. I would keep it in this room. If something happened to me, he would find it and know I understood part of what he'd tried to share with me, along with where to find the evidence of it—on his peninsula. The perfect place to experience and hide a heart. "God, keep both of us well enough Grandpa can hear everything from me when I return to New York. Or give him enough stamina to come here and find what I have written if I don't make it back," I prayed silently.

I placed the article for the *Times* in an envelope and sealed and addressed it. The copy of the article and my love story needed to be in something dark and weathertight so they couldn't be spotted where I would hide them in the peninsula's shelter. A place Grandpa would decipher from my cryptic note. He would devour every word but be especially interested in the story's ending, which I hadn't written yet. Because my ending looked like it would be the right one. Not the happy one I wanted. And I wasn't ready to give up enough blood to write that.

I held up Reed's article. "Did you read this too?" I asked Chastity. She shook her head. "Why not?"

She pointed to the gold pen. "I knew if you were going to truly write something from your heart, you would use that. And you did."

"My grandfather would love you. And you him." I rose from the chair, stuffed the copy of my story I hoped to finish and the article into a dark sock I would hide at the peninsula when Chastity wasn't with me. With it, Grandpa's gold pen, the *Times* article, and the one I would carry, clasped in my hand, I opened the door much as Randy Reed had for me the night before—a sliver barely wide enough to peer through.

"Are you acting out one of your stories?" Chastity stood behind me.

I scrutinized the parking lot before I turned to her. "Yes, a story that isn't fully written yet. I want it to have a happy ending."

She did too. I could see it in her eyes. "Write it that

way, Jim."

I tried to grin, but it was weak. If I wrote the ending to this story on my own, Dwayne would be history and Chastity mine. I wouldn't do that unless she wanted it that way. Her happy ending had to be happy whether it was with me or not.

Chapter 11

Halfway across the parking lot from my hotel room to the car, Chastity stopped walking. "You should call your grandfather before we go to my house."

"What?" I paused beside her and gaped at her expression of complete sincerity.

"You need to," she added.

I wanted to ask her how she could know such a thing, but I didn't. That her curls were Grandpa's favorite color, and she had introduced me to his peninsula, told me some sort of connection existed between them. The sort I couldn't explain and found difficult to believe in but chose to trust.

"I could, I suppose. But we have a lot to do for the wedding, and I promised you…"

"It's important." Again, Chastity's expression revealed absolute sincerity. "Jim Turner the famous author can help me plan a wedding, but the Jim Turner who wrote that story I read in your hotel room is tied to his grandfather. That connection is a thing of beauty you can't let slip away. And I don't want it to."

I wasn't sure what to say to such an unbelievable, mystifying, intuitive, and sensitive woman. I took her hand and veered her toward the lobby.

"You sound tired," Grandpa said to my greeting when I reached him by phone. He sounded tired as well.

"Late night," I responded while wondering if I

should return to New York after all. He sounded more frail than he had when I left for Grove.

"You want to talk about what you're writing?" he asked. He knew nothing about what I had written since coming here and asked because my stories were what we mostly talked about. I wasn't sure how to put into words what I had written with the gold pen. And he didn't need to know my interview with Reed really could cause people to end up dead. Maybe it already had.

"Not exactly," I said.

He was quiet for a moment. "Be careful, then." He rightly understood I had met with either the ex-con or Reed the snitch. He didn't sound afraid, though the warning was there. As always, Grandpa knew things. It was as if he held a winning poker hand against his chest, waiting for everyone else to make their choices before he showed them the end of the story. "But that isn't what you need to talk about, is it?"

My breath seeped out of me. How I wished he was here so we could talk face to face like we always did. If it wasn't for his failing health…and Hitler…I would fly Grandpa here now. "You're right," I finally said. "It's the peninsula."

"Who is she?"

I wanted to ask him the same thing, and about his experience here, but I knew he wouldn't tell me. If his peninsula encounter had been nothing more than a tale, he would have told it to me years ago. He sent me here to discover it on my own…and to write about it. "She calls herself Chastity." I glanced over my shoulder to where she sat. No, to where she had been sitting. Spotting only an empty chair, I gave the lobby a frantic scan until I spotted yellow. Blonde curls, blue eyes, and long legs sauntered around the room looking at everything, though the area contained nothing of great appeal.

"The peninsula is where it happened to me. And to her." Grandpa shared more than he had yet about his story.

It happened to her also? There was hope that Chastity would experience what I was? She would feel the same way I felt?

"Tell me what happened to you there," Grandpa interrupted my emotional whirlwind.

I began to tell him. But unlike a crime writer, I spoke words which flowed with color, breezes, and the aroma of lemons and flowers. Every facet of Chastity spilled from my heart and into the telephone. By the time I finished, her essence filled the lobby and probably Grandpa's house.

We remained quiet. He was no doubt reliving his peninsula experience while I watched mine tour the lobby.

"Are you writing all of this?" Grandpa asked.

"With your pen."

"Then you're writing my story as well."

"I had a feeling I had written yours along with mine, Grandpa, but only the essence of it. I would like some details. I would love to hear what happened to you."

He cleared his throat. "It's still happening, son. It's a story that never ended…" *Yet.* I heard the waver in his silence. Was that why he wanted me to write it? To bring it to a close? A happier ending than the one he now lived? No wonder he urged me to come here, to find my hidden piece that was so much like his. If he had turned it over to Jim Turner the crime writer, I would have annihilated the characters in Grandpa's story and prematurely sealed it with "The End." But this Jim Turner…

I glanced around for Chastity again. Somehow she had sensed this about my grandfather and me. Did she understand I couldn't finish my story unless he was in it too? Did she want the same happy ending I did, and that's why she insisted I call him? I spotted her chatting with Kevin, who had resumed his position behind the counter, his face bright red with a sheen of perspiration glowing in the lobby light.

"You got my note?" Grandpa asked, drawing my attention away from Chastity and Kevin.

"I did. I'm not really sure I know what you think I do."

"You will never know it if I tell you. Just write, son, and live. You will know."

Kevin raised and extended his arms as if he was describing something of enormous size to Chastity. He was probably exaggerating. Girls like Chastity brought that out in guys like him. And me. Probably all men.

"I have never written without a carefully outlined plot before. Writing from…"

"…the heart?" Grandpa finished for me. "You may never write this way again the rest of your life, but you have to this one time." For him and for me. My squeaky-clean inner voice had said the same thing.

"I'm afraid of how things might end," I blurted. "I can't stand the thought of losing Chastity. In fact, I won't stand for it."

"There are a lot of can'ts and won'ts that will keep you from her, and all of them come down to what loving her really means for you." His words hit me like a bucket of ice water dowsing a flame I wanted to keep lit.

"It wasn't Grandma you met in Grove, was it?" I bit my lower lip so hard, I tasted blood. If he said it was her, and he married and lived the story he never told, I had hope. For two out of the three heroes in my story ended up with the woman they loved.

"Your grandmother was never in Grove."

"Mountain Grove," I corrected him, my voice carried an edge.

"Grove, son. Stay there until you finish the story. And be careful." With that, Grandpa said he loved me and disconnected. It wasn't just life and limb he warned me to be careful about, it was also my heart. But more than anything, he meant Chastity's wellbeing and heart.

I stood with the handset cradled against my ear, the sound of the dial tone taking the place of Grandpa's voice. Grandma was never in Grove, and apparently my grandfather had never left it. He handed me a far greater mystery than any I had ever written, giving me the writing instrument and nothing else. Except for the word "love" and the assurance that I would know.

Chapter 12

Chastity joined me when I at last tore myself from the telephone. We stepped outside the hotel lobby but went no farther.

"How was your talk with your grandfather?" She looked up at me.

"Hard. Good, but hard." I pretended to study the scenery so she couldn't see how difficult our conversation had been. Or how much I wanted to be there and here at the same time and put a happy ending on both. "He said to be careful." I intended that to sound humorous and lighten the atmosphere, but she gasped.

"Oh." She clapped her long fingers over her mouth then slowly lowered them. "Kevin said the same thing. He told me an enormous hunk of a man was looking for you earlier, and you should watch out for him."

"Enormous like this?" I raised my arms the way Kevin had while talking to Chastity, then lowered them. Mocking Kevin did no one any good.

"Exactly like that. Who was it, Jim? Do you know?"

Reed? Clyde the ex-con I told Seth I wouldn't speak to? Someone worse? "Probably a fan of my books," I lied. "All sorts of people want my autograph." I glanced through the glass door into the lobby to where Kevin stood behind the counter watching us. "Come on. We have work to do."

Once I locked Grandpa's pen along with the copies

of my story and the article in my trunk alongside Chastity's bicycle, I took my time driving us to her home, twisting my neck and straining my eyes as I looked in every direction. I should have forced Reed to turn on a light last night, so I could recognize at least him.

"Why did you park so far away?" Chastity frowned down the long block between where I stopped my car and her house.

"Exercise," I lied. "A writer doesn't get enough of it." What this writer really needed was a bird's-eye view of who might be in the vicinity before either of us set foot outside this car.

She frowned. "Okay…well, I guess I can ride my bicycle while you trot along beside me."

"Sure. That's a good idea," I lied again. Within seconds, I hauled her bicycle from my car's trunk, leaving everything of mine behind. "Let's hurry. We have a lot to do, and a short run will be good for me." How many lies was that now? Three in a matter of minutes? Four?

"I had no idea you were so enthusiastic about exercise or my wedding."

In truth, I despised both. "Very enthusiastic. I'm ready if you are."

Chastity's cheeks flushed pink. "I was thinking the same thing."

The most gorgeous woman I had ever seen couldn't possibly be thinking the same thing I was.

She nibbled her lower lip. "I am ready when you are."

My heart hammered. I stared into eyes bluer than the sky. Once again, I would be an easy target if I were a fictional character in some thug's crosshairs. She would be planning my funeral instead of me planning her wedding, unless I got a grip on myself.

"Walk with me, Chastity." I moved her bicycle to my left side so she could walk unhindered on my right. As closely as we could without touching, though on the inside I held as tight to her as I could. We didn't talk, either, but in my mind, I rehearsed a thousand ways to describe the depth of my feelings for her and ask if she felt the same. If this was my story, I would throw her to the ground and cover her with kisses…as soon as she assured me I was the only man for her.

My heart cavorted wildly in anticipation. My skin tingled as I inwardly repeated my confession and question, every nerve longing to press her close. *She loves me…she loves me not…* We were within yards of her house. *She loves me…she loves me not.* Surely she loved me, yet the words lodged in my throat.

I silently admonished myself for cowardice and tossed my imaginary daisy aside. What sort of hero was I? I could talk to Reed, who may be dead by now, or to an ex-con, but I couldn't ask this slender blonde-haired beauty how she felt about me or confess my love to her.

By the time we reached the dirt patch she called a yard, perspiration glued my shirt to my skin. I gazed up at her balcony where her riot of fabric walls and curtains billowed out her opened windows and door. I drew in a bottomless breath of the heady aromas that enchanted me as they swept around where I stood. Where we stood. Chastity had placed her bicycle where she kept it then joined me, the two of us watching her essence being carried on the breezes. I needed a definitive answer from her. For her to say she didn't love me was better than losing her without ever asking. Just as writing about her with a heart broken by rejection was better than one bound in agony because I never knew.

Words began to string together in my mind once again. The question formed in my mouth. My legs trembled. I could never make it up her ladder in this weakened condition, causing her to believe Dwayne a far more capable man. I opened my mouth. It was now or never…

"Jim…"

I closed my mouth. My racing thoughts stilled. We locked gazes. I had never written a moment like this in any of my novels, but standing here felt as if this had been penned for me. And her. Foreign and familiar all over again.

"That was me in your story, wasn't it?" She gazed up at me.

My breath caught.

"The one I read in your hotel room. I knew you were writing about me the instant I began reading it. And about yourself. You're the hero in it, aren't you?" Her gaze said she hoped I was…or maybe she was afraid I thought I was, and she merely hoped to set me straight.

"Well, it's…" About three men and the women they loved.

"What happens? How will it end?" Chastity set a hand on my arm. Should I tell her what I feared might happen? Would it break her heart? Or would she be relieved?

"I don't know the ending yet." Clearly none of my crime novels were autobiographical. My heroes would be more forthright. Even Grandpa's heroes would love their heroines enough to be honest and die a thousand deaths to make sure their lovers' endings were the best possible ones…no matter what. "I know how I want it to end."

"Then there is hope…" Her eyebrows rose slightly. "Hope for…"

"For a happy ending. I trust you, Jim."

She loves me. In that moment, I sensed an indefinable, unspoken pact. She had a part in it and so did I, neither of us putting it into words or even trying to. How could someone describe a forever that might never be? Yet it would be, somehow.

She took my hand, and we climbed her rickety ladder. Upon reaching the balcony, I was swept into her wash of color, intoxicating aromas, and the wind as I followed her through her open door.

"It's so beautiful in here," I commented, then warmed at what I had said. "Criminally beautiful, I mean."

She laughed. Something about Chastity's world made the real world disappear. "I love it here," she said.

"I do as well." I should have said "love it" instead of "do." The look on her face told me she wouldn't have cowered away from a verb that expressed my true level of passion.

She disappeared behind one of her fabric walls to brew tea for us. Happy kitchen sounds carried on a chain of notes she hummed, while I absorbed her uncanny world, a world my grandfather would understand perfectly. I sank into her billowy chair, sipped something exotic she handed me, and let whatever it was we hadn't said that we didn't know how to say remain that way for the moment.

By the time I balanced my empty cup on my knee,

what we had left unsaid hung like an awkward silence. It was time to speak, say all the right things, and ask the pertinent questions. Her actions and the look on her face told me she felt as strongly about me as I did about her.

"Chastity," I began. Everything inside me wanted to drop down to one knee for this hallowed moment, but I stayed in my seat. "We have…"

Turbulence returned to her eyes. "Wait. Let me talk first."

I needed to swallow but couldn't. The words that expressed my profession of love gummed together like a wad in my throat. I needed to say them. This couldn't wait…

"You need to hear this. I hope you will understand…" she continued.

"Margie!" A woman's voice rose from the yard below.

Chastity's eyes widened.

I straightened in my seat. "Don't mind whoever that is. Probably some saleswoman for the war effort, searching for one of your neighbors." I wished whoever it was away from Chastity's house. The moment I had been waiting for was finally here, and the girl of my dreams seemed uncertain about something.

"Margie," the woman called again, her voice carrying through the open windows and door.

Chastity's face paled. "That's my mom." She clapped a hand over where she carried her unborn child and stared wide-eyed at the window.

"Your name is Margie?" I asked in a whisper. This young woman was far more a Chastity than a Margaret.

Chastity stole a peek at the ground below. "My dad is with her." She gave her billowy shirt and bright shorts

114

a dismayed grimace. "They can't see me like this. I need to change." A male voice—her father's, apparently—also called for Margie. She disappeared behind one of her fabric walls where a ruckus ensued I could only surmise was the shedding of her current outfit for something even more discreet. Parents or not, I still wished the two visitors away. They couldn't have chosen a worse time for a visit.

"How about this?" She appeared in front of me, her body completely hidden beneath a length of fabric loosely wound around her, the end draped over a shoulder. Had she torn down one of her material walls?

The panic on her face softened my irritation at her parents' interruption. "They will never guess you are hiding something," I assured her, though I knew from writing crime books that too much denial was a sure sign of guilt. "You look lovely."

She plastered a smile over her angst and stepped out to her balcony. "Mom, Dad." She waved down at them.

"There you are, dear." Her parents stood in Chastity's yard, their car parked where mine should have been. "We came by to see if you…" Her mother stopped when she spotted me behind their daughter. "Who are you? You aren't Dwayne. Are you?" She shielded her eyes from the sun.

I tugged on the back of Chastity's bolt of fabric. "Your parents haven't met Dwayne?" I whisper-hissed.

"Of course they have. You resemble him, that's all," she whispered over her shoulder.

"You mean because I'm tall." I didn't care for being confused with her missing fiancé.

"Dwayne is taller than you. But that's not the only resemblance."

Now I didn't care for her tone. Or for the tension which replaced the intimate communication she and I were about to share before…

"Margie, who is he? Please introduce us. And why are you wearing that…that material?"

"He's not Dwayne," Chastity assured her mom.

And assured me. I wasn't Dwayne. My earlier passion turned stony. For the third time, I willed her parents away so she and I could talk.

Completely unhindered by whatever she had wound around herself, Chastity eased over the railing and shinnied down her ladder, a feat that would have impressed me if I hadn't been struck so numb.

"Oh. You aren't Dwayne," her mother affirmed when I joined the three of them. This wasn't a real yard, Chastity's outfit wasn't real clothing, and I wasn't her real fiancé. I wrote fiction. I didn't want to live it.

"Mom, Dad, this is Jim," Chastity said, then swept her arm in their direction. "Jim, meet my parents, Hugh and Ruth Higgins. Most people call my father Pastor Hugh."

Hugh's height, Ruth's hair and eye color, and their slight builds combined into the perfect package of their daughter. So did their politeness as they greeted me, though I couldn't miss their concern as to what this complete stranger who resembled their future son-in-law was doing here.

I began to babble, hoping to assure them, me, and Chastity that I truly did belong here. "I am a writer visiting Grove. Chastity needed some help, so I…"

"His full name is Jim Turner. He is a famous author of crime novels and the answer to my prayer for help with the wedding."

"Dwayne is still gone?" Ruth frowned.

"He will be back." Chastity stiffened in her sheath.

I stiffened as well at the way Chastity defended him.

"This is part of what Jim helped me with." Chastity extended one of our handwritten invitations I hadn't seen her pick up before we exited her house.

Her parents stood close and read it, moist pink collecting in her mother's eyes.

"This is beautiful." Ruth clapped a hand against her chest.

"Jim wrote it."

Ruth gave me one of those kindly intuitive looks only mothers could. "Maybe you should write love stories instead of crime. This truly is wonderful."

"My editor would skin me." My face warmed. "I mean, I'm under contract for several more books."

"Which Jim will get back to writing as soon as he returns to New York," Chastity added.

The final blow struck. It felt fatal. She loved me not. I became deaf to their family chatter. Chastity loved Dwayne. Whom I resembled but wasn't.

How had this happened? I stared at the ground. Had I been a fool? Or been fooled? Clearly Chastity hadn't planned to tell me she loved me before her parents interrupted us. She was going to tell me she didn't and then ask me to leave. My skin turned icy in spite of the warm sun. The idea of a forever without her left me hollow inside.

"Let's talk somewhere more comfortable. How about lunch, you two?" Hugh asked.

I couldn't eat a bite. Nor could I stay here another minute.

"We don't have time." Chastity saved me by saving

herself, her hand pressed tight on her midsection. "So much to do. I have a long list of wedding items to attend to."

"You need to stay nourished," Ruth said like a good mother. "You look rather gaunt. And tired."

Chastity looked that and worse. Had she looked this poorly before they arrived but my passion had blinded me to her condition? Or had the shock of seeing her parents brought on this wan appearance? No matter who or what caused it or how much I hurt, I would do one last thing to help her and delay Ruth piecing together the evidence and suddenly detecting a grandchild behind her daughter's protective hand and yards of material. "Maybe you could bake twenty-six cupcakes for the wedding, Mrs. Higgins. Chastity is keeping refreshments simple because it might be windy on the peninsula."

"Her real name is Margie," Ruth corrected me, then turned to her daughter. "Have your reception at the church. I can make whatever you want, that way."

"Dwayne likes the outdoors." I nearly choked saying that. "Thank you, though. Could you handle drinks as well?"

Ruth's face lit up.

"Are you doing the ceremony?" I asked Chastity's father.

"I would love to," Pastor Hugh chimed in.

Her parents responded to being a part of their daughter's wedding with a hug, a huddle of three I had just created and secured for Chastity…Margie. Because this family needed to bond before things got rough when the baby could no longer be hidden.

I took a step back, the first of many I would take until I eventually ended up in New York. As Chastity had said I would.

"Paper, miss," a pre-pubescent male voice called from the sidewalk. Something thumped in the dirt behind me.

"I got it," I said more to myself than to Chastity or her family as I swiped it from the ground. They remained absorbed in a reunion they needed. I glanced down at Grove's newspaper as I carried it past two parents happily chatting with their daughter. I was losing Chastity to Margie before she even said "I do" to Dwayne. As I folded the paper back on itself to set it near her ladder, four words in bold print caught my attention. "Chastity To Be Married." My heart tightened at the wedding announcement I had written. My feelings instead of her words. I stared at everything that beat within my heart and everything I was about to lose.

As I read and re-read every bit of it, the word "cupcake" filtered through the air and over the thundering in my chest. I glanced at the Higgins family. Chastity's excitement at her wedding plans seemed a thin veneer over her earlier turbulence. But that could change with their support. I was in the way. She needed her parents now and would need them even more later.

"I have to go." I approached them, the newspaper tucked beneath my shirt. She should see one eventually, but not today. Not when it would remind her of me more than of Dwayne since I had written their announcement. And like my story, it described me, and her, and how I felt about her. "I need to call my editor about an article."

Ruth looked at me through her own indecipherable veneer. Had she and her husband seen this before? Some young man caught in Chastity's world of color, breezes, and smiles? A young man not meant to stay, no matter how much he loved their daughter? "You wrote a beautiful invitation," she said, as if fishing for what she really wanted to say.

"Let's all meet for lunch tomorrow, now that Ruth and I are taking over some of the wedding tasks." Hugh extended a hand, which I briefly shook.

"Sure," I lied, wondering if fibbing to a pastor was doubly wrong. "I will talk to you soon," I lied to the pastor's daughter. To Margie.

Chastity looked unsettled. I wallowed in utter misery. I would never have guessed that fulfilling my promise to help with her wedding would mean enlisting her parents and then leaving. The sidewalk blurred as I hurried to my car. A knot the size of New York swelled with excruciating pain in my chest.

"Lunch tomorrow," Hugh called. I raised my arm and waved, pretending to agree, but kept going. My feet staggered forward on a course that would take me all the way back to New York, exactly as Chastity had said.

Chapter 13

She loves me not. Instead of going straight to my hotel, I drove aimlessly around Grove. I wouldn't return to Chastity's house. She needed her parents more than she needed me, since Dwayne was her clear choice for a lifelong partner. Neither could I go to Grandpa's peninsula, since she and her parents would likely go there to view the site of her upcoming wedding.

My stomach knotted. Lucky Dwayne. From now on, every bad guy I wrote would look like him...and resemble me.

I circled my hotel, trying to muster enough self-control to call Seth and sound like a man instead of a blubbering, brokenhearted lover. He would be relieved to hear I was heading back to New York right away. The knot in my stomach lodged itself in my throat. Had I seen Chastity for the last time?

Unable to rally anything sturdier than a decision to tell Seth I was returning and then hang up, I stepped from my car into the hotel parking lot's radiant heat. I didn't care. They could burn me at the stake or send me naked to Antarctica. Nothing hurt like my heart. My broken heart. Taking a bullet there or anywhere in my chest couldn't possibly cause this much damage or pain.

Weighed to the ground with grief, I pushed through the lobby door. Kevin's "Urgent message for you, sir" didn't faze or deter me from my solitary trek toward the public telephone.

"It's urgent," he repeated at my side as I lifted the phone's handset.

"I told you, Kevin, it's never urgent. That's just the way my editor…"

"It isn't from your editor."

Grandpa? Fear displaced grief. I swiped the note from Kevin's hand and ripped it open.

"*Get out of there. Kill the article. It isn't even public news yet, and Reed is dead.*"

At the bottom was a New York telephone number which wasn't Seth's.

"Who…" I glanced up at Kevin.

"They didn't say, sir. But it was a man."

I nodded my thanks. Kevin rightly deduced I needed to be alone and headed back toward the counter.

"What about Wally?" I called to his retreating back. "Is he working later?"

Kevin turned. "No one has heard from him, sir." His grim look ignited a plume of panic inside. My skin turned clammy. My thoughts raced. Was Wally one of the bad guys or another of their victims? Either way, I should never have left Chastity. Unless staying away from her offered her the best protection. Since Wally and Reed were tied to me, she would be safer nowhere near me.

I fumbled to dial Seth's number, ignoring the one on the note. I stared at the warning to get out of Grove as the phone rang. And rang. Maybe Seth had made good on his threat to come here and was on his way. I glanced around the lobby and through its glass door, hoping to spot him. A steely hollowness crept through me.

"Be okay somewhere, Seth," I muttered as I hung

up, then dialed the number on the note.

An unfamiliar male voice answered with an impersonal, "*Times.*"

"This is Jim Turner, I…"

"You got my message."

"That's right, and…"

"We need to get you out of there quick. But first, where is the article you wrote for Reed? For the sake of your safety, I hope you mailed it."

"I haven't mailed it. Reed wanted to check what I wrote before I turned it over to anyone."

"He isn't calling the shots. Not now, of course, since he's dead, but he wasn't in charge before that either. We are. Well, I am, and you need to get that story in the mail pronto."

"Who are you?" No matter how tense this man made me, I found him irritating.

"How many copies did you make?" Impatient tapping sounds rose in the background.

"Two," I lied, since I had three. If I said I only had one, he would know I was deceiving him, since no author risked losing his work by typing a single copy.

"Send all of them to me," he said as if he knew I had more than two. "Do it quick. You will be safer that way."

"How about I send them to Seth?" Since I had no idea who "me" was. I was acting petty, but this guy annoyed me more than Seth did.

"Seth isn't around."

I didn't like the way he said that. "He told me he was coming to Grove, so he is probably enroute."

"Believe whatever you want."

Breathing became a struggle, and my mouth turned dry. My taunt to Seth about an editor's body washing up on the shore of the Hudson River was suddenly vividly clear. I would never write again if something had happened to him. Not crime novels or even wedding announcements.

"Here's the address to send the article copies to." The man rattled off a building number and street name in New York. "Just mark it to the *Times* and I will get it."

"What happened to Seth?" Four words I never thought I would say, even though I had fantasized someone would pose them to me on the days he was his most annoying.

"Just do as you're told." He hung up, leaving the dial tone humming in my ear.

I stood there, stupidly wondering if today was real or just an awful dream. A nightmare, actually. No Chastity, and no Seth... I clicked the receiver a couple of times and redialed Seth's office. His phone rang endlessly as I willed him to answer.

"Hello?" a hesitant feminine voice answered.

"Miss Olsen?" Seth's secretary never answered his phone.

"Mr. Turner?" She sounded relieved, a giddy sort of nervousness in her voice. "Have you spoken with Seth?" Miss Olsen didn't sound at all like herself. Her usual businesslike mannerism, the perfect complement for a volatile man like Seth, wasn't there.

"No, but I am looking for him. Did he head for Grove, by chance?" I silently begged for her to say yes.

I heard a sniffle and envisioned her dabbing at her eyes with a hankie. "Not that I know of." Her negative reply seemed swallowed in a sob. "He's not here at the office. His wife hasn't heard from him either."

I fumbled for words reassuring enough to wipe the

bleakness from the atmosphere. "Miss Olsen, he is somewhere, and we will find him. In fact, you can help by telling me everything you can recall about the last time you saw him. Plus, give me the name, number, and address of his contact at the *Times*."

Amidst more sniffles, she uncharacteristically related a shaky version of her most recent encounter with Seth, followed by a completely different name, address, and phone number for his contact than what the man who had referred to himself as the "*Times*" had given me a few moments ago.

"Did Seth say anything to you about Randy Reed?" I asked, meaning anything above and beyond what a secretary would be told as a matter of course.

Miss Olsen was astute. She knew exactly what I meant. I kicked myself for not appreciating her before now. When…not if…things returned to normal, I would spend more time talking to her than to Seth. "He stared out his office window at the Hudson River a lot." Which meant Seth was afraid. "He didn't want you talking to Reed." She paused. I knew there was more. "Mr. Turner…"

"I know. I will be careful and get out of Grove fast," I finished for her.

"Yes, that too…but also…"

"Don't worry. I know what to do. And what not to do."

"I was going to say, be careful who you trust." She said it as if she knew something. This shrewd woman, even though close to my age, teemed with more wisdom than Seth and I did combined. I had always sensed that, but now it mattered.

"This is advice you would give to Seth also?" Or had

she given it to him to no avail?

"Yes, Mr. Turner. It is, and I did." With a catch in her voice, she said goodbye and hung up.

Seth's disappearance, Reed's death, and the fake contact from the *Times*—there had to be a connection between the three, but I prayed there wasn't. Over the buzz of the third dial tone in my ear today, I also prayed Chastity would in no way be harmed or affected by whatever danger I had stumbled into. But more than that, I fervently hoped our meeting each other was a coincidence. Not something staged to distract and take the good guy down. The good guy and his editor.

Chapter 14

My gut churned with an ugly swirl of heartbreak and loss, turning me into a foreigner in my own skin. How could I live without Seth to taunt and Chastity to love? Their absences crippled me, but the idea of completely losing either utterly destroyed me. As I wallowed in agony, Grandpa came to mind. What about him? How far would Reed's enemies go to stop this article? As far as to threaten a harmless old man to get their hands on it?

I couldn't breathe. I pressed the telephone's handset against my chest to muffle the wailing dial tone so I could think. Criminals had agendas, but heroes made plans. And trusted very few, as Miss Olsen had warned me. Seth and my grandfather needed a hero; therefore, I needed a plan. Grandpa had lived for me and would die for me. I would do the same for him.

I felt Kevin's gaze boring holes into my back as I attempted to wrestle wild and erratic thoughts into a failproof strategy. First, I would call to check on and warn Grandpa. Next, I would pack and leave this hotel. Lastly, I would make a list of anyone in Grove I knew I could trust.

Resisting an urge to glance over my shoulder at Kevin, I dialed my grandfather's phone number.

"Randy Reed has been killed," I spewed as soon as Grandpa answered, the mere sound of his voice overwhelming me with relief.

He remained silent for a moment after my outburst. "I imagine your editor is having a fit about that," he stated. He portrayed a sense of calm, but beneath his casual observation, I detected a keen awareness of what this murder could mean for me.

"Seth would have a fit, you're right. He might have already done so, but I don't know. He is missing."

Another measure of silence. "A large persona like Seth's wouldn't be easy to hide. I say that as a warning to you, son. Had you sent him a copy of the article?"

"No. Reed didn't have one either, just me." The icy chill that raced up my back probably climbed my grandfather's spine as well. *Just me.* I was the sole possessor of what likely got Reed killed. The searing cold left its mark between my shoulders in the circular shape of a target. I glanced out the lobby door to where I had parked my car. No thugs lurked around it; therefore, the article and my story were both safe in the trunk. As safe as I was in an open lobby.

"You are calling to warn me to be careful," Grandpa interrupted my escalating fear.

"That's right." It came out raspy. "Reed's story hit a more dangerous chord than he or anyone, other than Seth, expected. Since my article never became public, that tells me Reed's enemy has been close all this time. Possibly posing as a friend." Or a lover. I stalled out. Like a car out of gas, I became a writer without words. The last item of my plan jumped to the top. Who could I trust around Grove? Not Wally. Or Kevin. But what about Chastity?

"I think we can eliminate the possibility one of Reed's friends did this." Grandpa's voice sounded far away. Miles from the bottom of the pit I had fallen into at the thought of Chastity being anyone or anything other than the sweet and gorgeous girl I had fallen for. "If someone close to Reed wanted to stop the story, he would have done it before you met the man or interviewed him." Grandpa paused. Probably waiting for me to agree. "Jim? You still there?"

No, I wasn't still here. The Jim Grandpa had watched grow up and succeed as a writer had ceased to exist the moment I stood on Mountain Grove's peninsula with Chastity. Now this new me, the one who fell in love and wrote with a gold pen, was rapidly fading from sight.

"It's unlikely Reed had a friend to begin with," I choked out, trying to sound normal. "He wasn't exactly congenial."

"Then if Reed's killer was anyone's friend or trusted acquaintance, they would be Seth's…"

"Or mine," I finished for him. "Or someone's at the *Times*." I staggered through the list of possible candidates, saying each one out loud for Grandpa, including Wally and the stocky woman who warned me I was being watched. I added the man who posed as Seth's contact at the newspaper, casting doubt on all of them…except Chastity. I omitted her name. To face that she didn't love me felt devastating. To think she might have playacted her part in our brief time together was unthinkable.

I waited for Grandpa to jump on one of the names I had suggested, but instead, he let out a series of tsks. "Son, the crime writer in you knows how to narrow that list. But the Jim I have spoken to since you arrived at Grove knows exactly what chord Reed's story probably struck. And who that chord belonged to."

I tried to swallow. No matter how much I wanted the motive to be greed, betrayal, the sale of business or military secrets, or even murder, I knew something far more powerful than all those combined could have cost Reed his life.

"The chord was love," I finally said. "A man might shoot someone who trespasses on his land or robs him, but he will destroy the one who in any way threatens the woman he loves." I understood the depth of that passion. Right or wrong, every ounce of me wanted to defend the girl with the blonde curls and blue eyes I had given my heart to. Hadn't I been willing to help her plan her wedding to another man? Hadn't I helped hide her pregnancy from her parents? I had even kept my mouth shut when I wanted to tell her and the world how much I loved her. Now, I would willingly risk my own life to cling to the belief I could trust her. But I wouldn't risk my grandfather's life. Never.

"If the chord was love, the deserter is the one who is trying to stop the story," I stated. "Not Hitler."

"That's my guess. That man gave up everything he had to save her. Now someone else has threatened to expose her, so he is viciously protecting the woman he treasures."

I pondered Reed's enemy. My enemy now. "That man is a pro at all things evil," I muttered. "He was well trained in how to execute harm."

"Yes, but he is also passionate. You can't teach that. Nor can fidelity to a cause ever stir a man to the depths fidelity to a woman can. Close, but a man gives his devotion to one and himself to the other."

Before coming to Grove, I would have dismissed such a statement. In fact, I had, countless times. Grandpa had faithfully seeded our conversations with examples of the power of loving someone, none of them taking root—until now.

"I wrote the deserter all wrong in our story," I practically gasped the revelation. "I barely skimmed the surface of his motivation to live, die, or kill for the one he loves." My heroic plan suddenly shifted again. "I am leaving Grove immediately and returning to New York. I will fix the story there, rewrite Reed's article so it is palatable for the *Times* but reveals the deserter's motives rather than exposing his crimes, and look for Seth." If the deserter was searching for me next, he would find me protecting my grandfather and salvaging my editor. Hopefully I would have time to show Hitler's ex-soldier my rewrite before he did anything rash. Of course, by the time I finished with all of that, Chastity would be married. Possibly gone from Grove. Leaving me uncertain as to whether I could have trusted her. I stifled a moan too deep for words. "In the meantime, I want you to go into hiding, Grandpa. Pack a bag and…"

"You can't write what you don't know, son. You are only halfway up the mountain. If you leave Grove now, you will never know what the top is like." Grandpa meant my unfinished business with Chastity. Omitting her from my suspect list and immediate plans must have exposed the gaping hole in my life.

"But if I stay here, something could happen to you like it did to Seth."

"A far worse catastrophe in Seth's life is that he wasn't really living to begin with. I have lived, son, and I haven't stopped. It's your chance now. Don't return too soon. And if your editor is fine somewhere, as I hope and pray he is, what you learn in Mountain Grove might benefit him." Grandpa's breathing changed when he finished. Grove had brought something good to him. But not without a dire cost. I had only scratched the surface in his story as well as in the deserter's. They knew something I didn't, because they had lived it.

Grandpa had been here and stood on Shale Lake's peninsula hand in hand with someone he left yet never really had. She would always be with him and he with her. No one could take that from him because whatever had happened to him and the one who always reminded him of yellow, he would carry that to the end.

I ran a hand down my face. If I stayed, I could end up watching Chastity marry instead of pretending from far away that she never did. What would the deserter do in my shoes? He would plug Dwayne if Dwayne was a threat to the girl of his dreams. But if Dwayne posed no threat, the deserter would pull the plug on his own happiness because it was best for the one he loved. In my opinion, he had proven himself capable of both.

"I will stay here but switch hotels, Grandpa. I will call you when I get settled." I paused as I considered everything else I would do. "I will still rewrite what is more than a story for all three of us. As for the article that cost Reed his life, it won't be about what the deserter did, but about why. It will be a glowing love story instead of a journalistic piece on crime." My throat clogged. I knew it was tears because this phone call's goodbye to my grandfather might be our final one. "You be careful. Find a hotel and stay there. Please."

"No need to worry, son. Hurry and get the article written. And walk out the ending for the story. Then get back to New York so I can read both."

I tried to swallow the lump in my throat. The

promise of "I will" got stuck with it, so I nodded.

"Goodbye, son. I love you."

This time I hung up. I couldn't stand to hear a dial tone in place of my grandfather's voice, nor did I want him to hear me cry. Or anyone to hear, for that matter. I escaped from the lobby, keeping my back to Kevin, and hurried to my room.

After three blurry-eyed, unsuccessful jabs at the lock with my key, I swiped away tears with my arm. With the key steadied in one hand, I grabbed the knob with the other. Which turned before I even inserted the key. Had I left the door unlocked? Standing to the side, I gave the door a shove. It swung inward, giving me a panoramic view of what looked like the aftermath of a hurricane. My beloved typewriter lay on the floor, its keys crushed as if a giant had put his foot through them. My bed was stripped, my suitcase emptied, the carpet marked with smashed and broken toiletries. Even my veiled note to my grandfather lay on the floor wadded and torn.

Besides myself, the only things that survived this attack were my article, my story, and thankfully Grandpa's gold pen I had locked in my car's trunk. I stepped cautiously into the room and surveyed it for what I could salvage and came away with a single change of roughed-up clothing. With them and my battered typewriter under my arm, I left the door to my room wide open, the key and a note regarding the final bill on the dresser, and headed to my car.

Chapter 15

The dilemma I found myself in revealed pretty quickly that it was far easier to write a clever good guy than to be one. My plan changed again as soon as I locked myself and my few possessions inside my car.

"I need a different vehicle," I dictated out loud, hoping to at least sound like I was in control. "A car no one will recognize." I checked the parking lot for anyone who might follow me, started my car, then headed to the city.

The area of Chicago where I exchanged my rented car for a completely different one offered everything I would need—a new typewriter, paper, ink for Grandpa's pen, a small travel bag, extra clothing, and more toiletries. I considered other items my fictional heroes would buy—a gun, a change of hair color, a fake beard or mustache—but I knew my best weapon had always been the right word. The right story and article, in this case. Which might save me from Hitler's deserter's desperation.

Step number two of my plan was to stay in the city for the day. Chicago's crowds and noise felt familiar and comfortable, its swarming activity the perfect cover to achieve anonymity. In this chaos I could complete step number three—sit and write.

Hustle and bustle offered my attacker the same invisibility it provided me, so I chose a public parking lot with a back wall I could park close to, leaving me only three sides to watch. Once situated, I settled into the driver's seat, readied paper and Grandpa's pen, and wrote.

The words flowed. Reed's intent of sensationalism and wartime revenge vanished. My new article about the deserter boasted a true hero instead of a possible villain. It turned an obscure victim into a beautiful heroine. This tale had heart and was about the heart. I reviewed pages of beautifully written prose when finished. So different from the article I had typed out on my beloved typewriter. This one was true, the whole truth, and I intended Hitler's deserter to see it. Even if it was the last thing I did.

I checked into another hotel in a small town not far from Grove. Night had fallen by the time I reached my new room. For the first time since I had begun traveling as an author, I approached it completely alone. No Grandpa, no notes from him or calls from Seth. No one in the world knew where I was. To the best of my knowledge, no one had followed me all day.

Thinking like one of the good guys in my novels, I chose a second-story room with its door to the outdoors, not one accessed from within a long, narrow, dimly lit hallway. My plan was built on safety, but as I stood on the balcony before entering my room, safety lost its significance. Another balcony rose from my recent memories. One which circled a decrepit building where the only woman I would ever love made her home.

I drew in a deep breath, her lemony fragrance nowhere around. Before morose thoughts could swallow me alive, I unlocked the door, then latched the double locks behind me, something else I had specifically looked for in a room. Setting my belongings on the bed, I walked to the far window at the back of the room and peered around its curtain to the ground below. I could escape through this if I had to, and survive a two-story drop. My gut cringed. How many times had I fantasized about Seth toppling from his second-story office window? Shame on me.

Utter aloneness pressed in on me. The harrowing chill of what might have happened to Seth…and what might happen to Grandpa…terrified and steeled me at the same time.

I set to work so I wouldn't listen to the distressing voice or the glum beating of my lonely heart. This room didn't have a desk, but the dresser's top was long and deep enough for me to work at. I set my mangled typewriter next to my new one on the shiny surface, my long-time writing companion's smashed keys bringing up more sorrow and a gruesome reminder of the damage someone out there could do. And had done, at least to Reed.

Once situated at the new typewriter, I typed two copies of my new article about Hitler's deserter, one to carry on me, the other to leave in this room. Either I or it could be ransacked, so hopefully it would end up in the deserter's hands in one way or the other. I would mail the original to Miss Olsen with strict instructions to place it into no hands other than Seth's…when he resurfaced. He might not understand a love story, but maybe my trip to Grove could turn into his "someday" as it had mine. Just as Grandpa suggested.

Someday, son, something will send your moral compass into a tailspin. Gravity will vanish, and you will fling your guards aside. What has always been singular vision will suddenly become kaleidoscopic. When that happens, grab this pen and write. With blood as your ink, write your heart on the page.

And maybe his current experience would help him recognize my ink as blood and the heart as that of Hitler's deserter. I sat for a moment. Seth had to survive. I couldn't imagine life without him.

Once finished, I set my story and Grandpa's pen in front of me. Everything I had written about the three heroes, especially Grandpa and the deserter and the women they loved, rang true as I read it. But I saw it with new eyes. These three stories in one, especially their parts, were far more than something to write about. They truly were life on a page. Once again, just as Grandpa had said. Unlike the two of them, I had yet to fully experience that level of life, but I had stayed in Grove as Grandpa encouraged me to. I had a mountain to climb which somehow involved Chastity. With hints of that life stirring inside, I picked up the gold pen and began to write again.

I woke up to morning noises outside my room and found myself sprawled like an accident victim across my bed's blanket. Disheveled and groggy, I noted Grandpa's pen had somehow survived an exhausted sleep and remained gripped in my hand. Craning my head, I spotted pages of my story strewn across my dresser's top. I must have written myself into oblivion. I sat upright and rubbed too little sleep from my eyes, then made my way to where I had sat the night before and gathered the pages to read.

When finished, my heart beat like a hero's, and Grandpa's pen felt more like a weapon than a writing instrument. I had captured the past, present, and future in one moment. Like the eternity Grandpa said was as brief as a fantasy but still lived on. I had stood inside a heart and written everything there, even the things that weren't…because the heart had willingly let them go, keeping the empty chambers for eternal memories.

At the end of my tale, I stared at the last word— Chastity. There were probably other men who loved a woman the way I loved her, but I could only think of the two I had written about.

I placed my finger on her name. Step number four of my plan. Find her. And learn the truth.

I gathered the article I had originally written for the *Times*, along with its copies, and put all into an envelope I would take with me to destroy. Then I rounded up my previous night's work and put each into the envelopes I had purchased, addressing one for Miss Olsen. After I bathed and dressed, I tucked the story and my copy of the article into a narrow leather pouch I had purchased which attached to a harness I wore beneath my shirt. Leaving one copy of the article behind, I left the hotel. To find her.

Chapter 16

The leather harness holding the pouch beneath my shirt did nothing to suppress my heart's hammering, my shirt pulsing with each beat. No longer did I flitter between *She loves me* and *She loves me not*. Chastity didn't love me. But I loved her. And the men in my story loved to the death. Even if the woman who held each of their hearts was an enemy. Like the deserter's lover he risked everything for. Like Grandpa's? I still didn't know.

With Chastity's wedding only a day away, I imagined her to be in one of two places—her mother's house to help with the baking or at the peninsula. Disregarding that inkling, I drove to her house anyway, where I found everything closed up tight. No open door or windows. No colorful fabric or exotic fragrance carried by the breeze to the yard and street below. My knuckles turned white as I gripped the steering wheel and gazed up to the balcony where she should be. Chastity was gone? Really gone, since she never closed up her house, as far as I knew? I clenched the steering wheel tighter.

With no idea where her parents...or Dwayne's mother...lived, I sped to Shale Lake, rolled out of my car, and barreled to Grandpa's peninsula. I prayed I would find her there, safe and alone. But I knew I could find her with Dwayne, or with her parents at the very least. What I found stopped me in my tracks. Far worse than anything I had dreaded, the tip of Grandpa's peninsula was roped off with signs announcing Chastity's upcoming nuptials posted around it: *Site of Margie and Dwayne's wedding.*

I stared at their names and the date and time below them. Still scheduled for tomorrow, late in the day. Numb, I took in a cluster of chairs, a trellised arch in front of them, vases for flowers at its sides, and a separate seat for a musician. I felt sick. Dwayne couldn't possibly love her the way I did.

Stepping around the area reserved for her ceremony, I made my way to the peninsula's tip. I had to breathe. I had to think. Almost as intoxicating as Chastity's home, I stood there and drank in the sensations of the breeze, the gentle lap of water, and the sparkle of the waves that rolled my way. Medicinal. Surreal. "Beautiful," I finally said. This time my face didn't redden. It was true. I was in love and this serene spot was magically beautiful. Even if the object of my affection turned out to be an enemy.

Refusing to dwell on that possibility, I pondered tomorrow when Chastity—Margie—would stand here and hold hands with Dwayne. I closed my eyes against the thought and tried not to imagine a man even taller than I was but whom I resembled standing where I did now.

A man appeared in my mind anyway. He wasn't taller, though. He was my height and weight, with the same straight brown hair, but in odd clothing. "Grandpa?" My eyes fluttered open. He had been here. Exactly here. Holding hands with... I tried to remember who I had just envisioned next to him. Someone...and yellow.

Wanting to hold onto the image, I dropped cross-legged to the ground and let the breeze brush against my face…our faces…Grandpa's was still there. He seemed so real.

"Who is she?" I whispered instead of asking who she was. They were here, close by, the story I was writing coming to life, and I was in it with him.

I waited for his response. The lapping of the waves tickled my ears as I listened. Then it came. "Love doesn't always say, 'I do.' The deepest love might never utter those words." Because out of that selfless depth, it was able to let go.

The vision of my grandfather grew stronger, standing where I had. He looked so much like me, but she… Her skirt billowed with the peninsula's breeze, their hands and gazes locked together.

I laid a hand over the leather pouch where the deserter's true article and our story lay. It had seemed so important, a day ago, to hide these in the peninsula's shelter where, if the worst happened, Grandpa could find them. As the images of him and whoever was with him faded, I understood Grandpa somehow knew what I had written. And he was pleased. Another thought shattered the peacefulness of that realization. Did that mean Grandpa was gone? Or that he was finally satisfied?

Sitting on the peninsula's tip, surrounded by wedding essentials, I found my plan returned with more urgency: Find Chastity. But I didn't move. I wouldn't until every sense of Grandpa faded. Once it finally did, I rose to my feet.

Everything in me wanted to rush to New York to find him, while that same devotion wanted to honor his last spoken wish for me. Stay and climb Grove's mountain. Live what he asked me to write.

Shale Lake's breezes soothed me, whereas Chastity's enticed me, both encouraging me to stay. I would for him. "Just be all right," I whispered to his absence. "And if you can, please hold on a while longer."

The urgency to find Chastity compelled me away from Shale Lake, but not before I put an end to a wrong story. Gathering my copies of the original article based on Reed's notes, I carried the antithesis to the deserter's love to the lake, where I cast them on top of its waves. I watched the water soak and then swallow into its depths what should never be told.

Sullen, yet relieved that my pen had done what it could to set one of my heroes free, I drove back to Chastity's house, which I found still silent and closed up. Like a morgue. Like someone on a honeymoon. I stared at a building that looked like I felt.

"Snap out of it, Jim," I admonished myself. Closing up and locking her house seemed more of a Margie decision than a Chastity one. Unless Chastity really had been nothing more than a plant to keep tabs on me while I interviewed Reed.

Leaving my car, I scrambled up a ladder that had always intimidated me, sailed over the balcony railing instead of slithering, and hammered on her door.

"Chastity," I fairly bellowed, then called for Margie when no one responded. I did the same at every window and the back door. Maybe Dwayne had returned early, and the wedding setup on the peninsula wasn't waiting for the ceremony but was instead ready to be taken down.

I slumped against the building's rough wooden front and slid to the balcony's floor, ignoring the pain. She was gone. Married, possibly. Mrs. Dwayne Something instead of Chastity. Men weren't supposed to cry, but I wanted to. Grandpa should never have sent me to this place. His peninsula gave and took the first and last love of my life. Being in Grove robbed me of valuable time with him. And my own foolish insistence that I interview Reed while here might have cost me Seth. My life had been so much simpler as Jim Turner, famed writer of crime novels. Those stories were black and white, straightforward, and typed instead of written by a broken heart.

I slumped lower. Tears rose behind my eyes and a sob pushed past the lump in my throat. My heart burst, and my eyes flooded. If I had Grandpa's pen in my hand right now…and didn't break it…the ink really would look like blood. But it would smell like lemons.

Indifferent to splinters, I leaned my head back against Chastity's outer wall. Had I lost the three most important people in the world to me? Some grandson, writer, and answer to prayer I turned out to be. If Hitler's deserter appeared in the dirt patch below, I would let him shoot me. No, I would throw myself over the balcony railing and pummel him for doing so heroically what I apparently couldn't. I buried my face in my hands.

"Hey, sissy, you Turner?" a gruff voice barked from below.

I froze. I had imagined the deserter's voice like that, deep like a foghorn. But I had also expected an accent. I peered above my hands, swiping humiliating tears from my eyes as I did. The largest man I had ever seen loomed like a giant below. Huge like a bull, without a bit of fat. Two bulls, maybe. I scrambled to my feet, glad a ladder that couldn't possibly hold him stretched between us.

Without that advantage, I had the chances of a pencil against Mount Everest.

"I'm Jim Turner." I tried to sound tough. Hard to sound and look the part in my nice, new clothing while his dirty undershirt sagged in all the right places to show off his muscles. His scruffy whiskers, wiry hair, and soiled pants made me feel as hardy as a china doll.

"Where's the babe?" The hulk looked to my right and my left and then at the rest of Chastity's house below.

"She is a lady, not a babe," I corrected him. "And she is no concern of yours." I gulped. "How do you know about her anyway? Who are you? Are you Randy?" I felt giddy with hope that this was Reed and he was still alive.

He looked bigger than I had estimated Reed to be in his dark motel room, but who else would be looking for me? I gulped again. This could be whoever did Randy in.

"Randy? What sort of name is that for a man?" He bellowed, but he wasn't really a laughing sort of fellow. If I lived, I would put a character like him in one of my books, since he far surpassed any bad guy I had ever contrived. "My name is Clyde. We was supposed to meet."

Clyde. The ex-con Seth wanted me to talk to so I wouldn't go soft and start writing romance novels.

"I cancelled that meeting. You are wasting your time here." My voice sounded birdlike compared to his tuba tones.

"My time?" Clyde bellowed again. "Of course my time is limited, if you get my meaning, but never wasted."

I read exactly what he meant in his harsh demeanor. Every second he was out of prison was an opportunity for him. The sort of opportunity he wouldn't waste and that could land him back in jail any minute.

"Your time would be better spent elsewhere," I told him. "I am sorry if my editor didn't make it clear that I wouldn't be interviewing you. I also apologize for whatever trouble you went to in finding me."

He guffawed. "You're easy to find."

My skin turned icy. Being easy to find was something I needed to fix, since Clyde and Reed had both chided me about it. "Look, now is not a good time. If you insist on meeting, how about later?"

"You got more crying to do?" He sneered. "We do this now. Though I was looking forward to seeing the babe."

"Leave her out of this." How did this hulk even know about Chastity?

"We never see nothing like her in the pen. I wouldn't have laid eyes on her ever, if it wasn't for some incompetent clerk who made a mistake. I got let out based on a technicality." Clyde widened his stance and crossed his beefy arms. "The cops are anxious to get me back behind bars, so I ain't gonna help them none by taking advantage of a pretty young thing like her. I got bigger things in mind. They know it. That's why they offered these ridiculous interviews with me. Clowns. Keeping me busy, so they can keep tabs on me in the little bit of time I have until some judge fixes their mistake, is a joke. But we won't let them know that, will we? I show up and you ask questions. Let them think I'm happy scaring people to death by bragging about all I've seen and done. They have no idea what I'm really up to or who I got connections with."

I swallowed. If Seth was here, I would wring his

neck in spite of how worried I was about him. Clyde was using me as a part of his cat-and-mouse game with the cops.

"You ready for my story? I got some pretty brutal experiences. My rap sheet will make your skin crawl."

So I had been told. Seth was an idiot to refer to Clyde as an ex-con. The cops knew, Clyde knew, and I could see that "ex" was on paper only. The "con" part was on Clyde for life like a tattoo, a map of every nasty thing he had seen and done. And was apparently still doing.

"I don't have anything to write with." I tried to sound indifferent, but Clyde bellowed again. Even his laugh was terrifying. I prayed no one would let a clerical error free him again.

"You don't need pen or paper," he spouted. "You won't ever forget what I tell you."

He was right, and I knew it. I really would wring Seth's neck next time I saw him, no matter what sort of shape he was in.

"I don't work that way," I said as boldly as I could. "I don't expect you to understand it, but I am responsible for every word I come by or share. I won't interview you without a way to record it."

Clyde had the keen criminal eye I wrote about but had never stared into. He probably catalogued my every weakness as his gaze cut through me like a knife.

"However…" I sputtered to free myself from his scrutiny. "There is one thing you can tell me that I won't need to write down."

His eyes narrowed and he gave me a short nod.

"Who could someone of foreign citizenry contact around here to knock another person off?"

"You mean a person with a big mouth that needed shut for good?"

My eyes widened. He meant Reed. I could barely squeak out a "Yes."

"You don't want to know." He stalked to the bottom of the ladder. I gaped down while he glared up. "Don't try to follow me." He knocked the ladder to the ground. For such a monstrosity of a person, he managed a near-perfect pivot as he wheeled toward the street. I didn't take my eyes off him as he walked to my car and thunked his knuckles on its trunk. My different car I should have parked somewhere else instead of foolishly right in front of Chastity's. "Something to think about…" He glanced back at me. "That editor of yours is as easy to find as you are." Then he was gone.

I shook from head to toe. Clyde had said "*is* as easy to find" instead of "was." Could he mean Seth was all right? And hiding somewhere? I felt giddy, shivering and shaking all at the same time. I collapsed against the wall and leaned there until the tremors subsided to general trembles. Reed had clearly been silenced. Yet Clyde didn't bother to suggest I could suffer the same fate by publishing what Reed had said. Nor did he mention my grandfather.

Keeping one eye on the direction Clyde had disappeared, I began to pace Chastity's balcony. Maybe I had misjudged Clyde by gauging him to be all brawn and no brain. He had effectively made my skin crawl with terror without relating a single one of his crimes or leaving me with a warning threat. Instead he had suggested only two things—Reed was murdered for his big mouth, and my editor who knew of the article was easy to find. Like I was. Clyde essentially told me I had a target on my back without saying it. He was far more a pro than a braggart. And he was right—the police underestimated him.

I picked up my pace so I wouldn't freeze with fear. I needed to mail my revised article to Miss Olsen, call Grandpa and pray he answered, and find Chastity.

I paused my march and peered at the ladder lying on the ground below, falling no longer my greatest fear. Chastity married, Seth easy to find, and Grandpa...I gulped...all far more terrifying in the wake of Clyde's laugh. I would drop from three stories to save the three of them. Instead of slithering over the railing one leg at a time and dangling by my fingertips, I grabbed its top board and leapt over it like a true hero.

"I'm coming," I yelled in my short free fall, and hit the dirt in a full sprint, stopping only long enough to prop Chastity's ladder back up where it belonged, because I hoped and prayed she was still here.

Chapter 17

I mailed the article to Miss Olsen first, then drove everywhere I thought Chastity might be. I did it without looking over my shoulder. Reed and Clyde had both made it clear I was easy to find, so why waste energy trying to hide? I returned to the peninsula first, then checked the newspaper office. After that I toured the downtown stores, the only flower shop I knew of, all with the hope Chastity was still in Grove. And still the sweet girl I had fallen for.

After a careful sweep through town, I ended up where I had first started upon arriving at Grove. It seemed years ago that I stood in the parking lot of the hotel that Seth…the *Times*…had chosen for me, feeling just as lost then as to which direction to go. I crept into the lot and parked at the side opposite the rooms. Should I begin here again? Stand on the pavement and spin in a circle until I decided which way to go?

I opened my car door the same moment the lobby door opened. The flash of light on its glass caught my eye…but the brilliance of yellow curls in the sunlight captured it. Chastity. I burst from my vehicle, and in a few speedy strides, I crossed the parking lot and skidded to a halt in front of her.

"You're here," we both gasped at the same time.

"Why?" I asked the same moment she did.

I vaguely indicated the parking lot while she pointed

toward my old room.

"That's not my room," I said at the same time she said, "That's no longer your room."

We stared at each other, enveloped in a cloud of lemony fragrance. I devoured her from her blonde curls to her sweet toes, pausing only at the cutest face I had ever seen. Beautifully cute, I had deemed her the first time I saw her, and she still was. With a slight flush dotting skin a little too pale.

"Are you all right?" I asked, more afraid for her than I was for myself. Surely that was the flush of an exhausted near-bride who was carrying a child, not the weariness of a spy who had finally located me. And certainly that was a look of relief that she had found me well, instead of relief that her job was over and I could be turned over to someone's thugs.

"Please don't think I came here looking for you because I'm tired and need your help." Her brows bunched into a concerned pinch above her blue eyes.

"But you should be here asking for my help. I'm sorry. I shouldn't have abandoned you. It's just that once your parents showed up…"

She touched my arm, her fingertips warm and cool at the same time. "About that," she began.

"I like your parents." I tried to save her from saying what I didn't want to hear. "They are wonderful people."

She nodded and tugged her lower lip between her teeth. "They liked you, as well. My father still plans on lunch together today. You don't have to, though. I have already made excuses for you. For me. For us." Her sentences came out choppy, her lower lip tugged in between each one. "It looks like you are planning to leave anyway. That's what the desk clerk just told me.

He said you left your key and were gone."

Desk clerk? She didn't say Kevin. I squinted, trying to see through the glare of daylight on the lobby's glass door. It blinded me. If Wally was in there, he could see me, whereas I couldn't see him. I took Chastity by the arm and drew her away from the door to a far corner of the building where we couldn't be seen. Once there, I kept my hold on her. She couldn't possibly be anyone's enemy. Not with a face like that, nor with the tired and worried look which darkened it.

I was in danger, and she could be also. Or she could be dangerous... Instead of flipping between my old *She loves me* and *She loves me not*, I switched to "She can be trusted" and "She cannot." Time was of the essence if Wally was in the lobby. I had to choose, and I chose to trust her. Foolhardy or not, I felt myself inch up a bit higher on Grove's mountain.

"I had to leave this hotel. And I had to get a different car. Not because I was returning to New York." I swallowed. "Well, that's not completely true. Yesterday, I thought..."

"I'm so sorry about yesterday, Jim."

Everything I was about to say vanished. She was sorry about yesterday? She hadn't meant to dismiss me so handily in front of her parents? Her allegiance wasn't solely to the absent Dwayne? Maybe she did love me...

I gave myself a mental slap. "Speaking of yesterday, I saw the peninsula. You were busy." I sounded stiff, like a male Margie. Slightly gruff, like a thin Clyde.

Chastity looked pained and glanced to the side. Was that a tear I spotted?

I backpedaled. A hero loved, no matter what. If I died doing it, I would love Chastity the way she needed me to. I fumbled for the most appropriate topic I could think of. "Do you have a flower girl or ringbearer? An usher?" I couldn't believe I even knew those terms, but wherever my memory dredged them up from, I was glad they were there, because she needed help with her worries.

"I suppose a flower girl would be nice…" She looked puzzled, tired, but her tear dried. "I won't need an usher, with so few coming." She gave me an almost desperate look. "You will be there, right?"

I should be there for her, but I would rather be there with her. Even if it made me an easy target for Reed's killer.

"You could stand with me," Chastity muttered.

"What? You mean like a Maid of Honor?"

"My very best friend."

"Don't you have a bridesmaid?" I asked.

"No."

"I…won't wear a dress." I felt like an idiot. But if there was a chance I would die, I wanted to go looking like a man. A heroic man. Or a groom standing in Dwayne's spot when she repeated her vows. Not behind her clutching a spray of flowers.

"You could wear the shirt I sewed last night using the same fabric I made my wedding dress from."

"You did that for me? Last night?" She was thinking of me while I was writing about her?

"I want you there with me." She gazed down.

"I would love to stand up there with you," I said with far too much honesty in my voice. "If I can't be the groom, I can at least be a brides-man instead of a bridesmaid."

Warmth shone in her eyes when she looked up.

"You will always be my brides-man, Jim. Always and forever." She squeezed my hands.

We both stared at our clasped hands, her naked ring finger amidst her other heavily ringed ones almost shouting, "I am waiting for Dwayne, for his promise—I am keeping myself for him only."

I touched the empty place where a diamond should be. If Chastity was my girl, she would be sporting a rock so big guys like me would stay away from her.

"No wedding or engagement rings," Chastity said. "I assume that is what you are wondering. Dwane suggested we get tattoos. I will have a D on my ring finger, and he is having a C tattooed onto his."

"You're what?" I practically bellowed, fascinated and horrified at the same time. "You can't do that. I mean, are you sure?" What would her parents think?

Her cheeks tinged pink as she stared at her stark finger.

Surely, I could come up with a word less discourteous than "outrageous." Some writer I was. "It's just that a tattoo is pretty bold." Unless you were a sailor. "If something happens to Dwayne, you will have to wear gloves the rest of your life." My dark and slimy side didn't have to suggest that I buy her a pair as a wedding gift. White gloves with a tiny pearl button at the wrist. It was purely my idea, and even if I carried the wrapped gloves with me the rest of my life, I would buy them.

She gave me a wide-eyed stare. Maybe for suggesting Dwayne's demise. Then she burst into laughter. Gales of laughter. The kind that brought happy tears to her eyes as she doubled over. One side of my mouth quirked upward. I offered a nervous titter to her full-blown gaiety.

"You're so funny, Jim." She clasped her stomach and straightened, wiping joyous tears from her face with the other hand. "My father is probably looking for us…for me…" Eyes which had been smiling looked suddenly horrified. She clapped both hands over her belly. "Ouch," she whooshed in a gasp. Her face paled and moisture beaded across her forehead.

"Are you okay?" I grabbed hold of her. Clearly she wasn't. "Chastity," I said as she slumped in my arms.

Chapter 18

"Are you family?" The hospital receptionist detained me at the front counter.

"No."

"Can you tell us her name or any of her medical history?"

"I brought her here and I simply want to see her. Which room have they taken her to?"

"We have a strict policy about patient care, and it involves family members first. Even in the worst of family dynamics, we have found close relatives know the most and are the ones the patient most often asks for. So can you tell me who she is related to?"

"Her father is a preacher in a nearby town. Hugh and Ruth…" I drew a blank as to their last name.

"Pastor Hugh? Why didn't you say so? Take a seat, I know how to contact him."

I glanced at my watch. Her father wouldn't be at home, he would be at Chastity's house waiting for her. "I doubt you can find him. He came to Grove to meet his daughter for lunch."

With the phone cradled between her shoulder and ear, and her finger poised in the dial, the receptionist raised an eyebrow at me. "Pastors are always available." She dialed a number and, sure enough, began to talk to someone. "He and his wife will be here soon. All you have to do is call a pastor's church and they can contact him. In case you aren't familiar with such things."

"I'm an answer to prayer," I defended myself from her skeptical look, then regretted it. "Sorry. I'm worried. Can you at least tell me how she is?"

"Who are you and what is your relationship with the good pastor's daughter? Besides being someone's answer to prayer."

"I am Jim Turner, and I…"

"The writer?" She gaped.

"Yes. And I'm a friend. I'm helping with the wedding."

The receptionist pinched her lips together and eyed the direction they had taken Chastity. "I heard you were in town. Welcome to Grove." Her cheeks picked up pink highlights. "As for the wedding you are referring to, Pastor Hugh's daughter is marrying Dwayne…"

Did I detect a hint of distaste? "Do you know him?" I ventured.

She shrugged. A one-shoulder shrug. The worst kind. "He isn't here?" she asked with a slight edge.

"No. He will be back for the wedding." Supposedly.

"I see. He hasn't been around much. And since he isn't here now, I might let you go back to see her in his stead…" She tapped her fingers. "Go on back, since you are you. Room Number104."

I never ran, in spite of my lie to Chastity that I did it for exercise. I was a walker, and a writer who paced while chewing on story lines. But before the receptionist could change her mind, I vanished down the hall and skidded to a stop in front of Room 104. I raced to a bed where a face as white as the sheets lay in slumber, eyes closed. Should I say her name? Hold her hand? Kiss her like I was a prince in a fairytale, so she would awaken?

"Are you family?" A nurse pushed past me to Chastity's bedside, her hands loaded with shiny instruments.

"Friend," I said instead of introducing myself as Prince Charming. "The receptionist sent me back while we wait for her parents," I added to a look ready to oust me from the room.

"When her real family comes, step outside," she said in a business-like tone.

"Yes, ma'am," I muttered.

Before the nurse finished with whatever she was doing, Pastor Hugh and Ruth rushed into the room. Their expressions went from terror at their daughter's comatose whiteness to shock at my presence. I nodded and slipped from the room without a word, then sequestered myself in a corner of the waiting room. Dwayne would likely be summoned. As he should be. After all, I was a complete stranger to them and their daughter, other than my renown as a cold-blooded killer of fictional hoodlums.

Each time a tall young man approached the receptionist's desk, I tensed and listened closely for a request for Chastity's room number...or Margaret's. I would leave if one of them did. Once here, Dwayne would take over for a wedding that would surely be postponed.

The few tall men who came also went, none asking for Chastity. I paced and occasionally stared out the large front window at the parking lot. How was she? Who was she? Should I even be here?

"Jim?"

I whirled around and faced Hugh.

"Margie is asking for you." His taut expression told

me he had more to say. Had he learned about his daughter's pregnancy? Or was he upset because she asked for a near-stranger who abandoned her yesterday?

I didn't ask. I raced to her room where her mother stood at the bedside holding Chastity's hand.

"Jim." Chastity smiled, her face still pale. "I'm so sorry. I have ruined everything."

"Hardly," I said, holding myself back from taking her other hand.

"No, I did. By not eating and drinking enough." She omitted "for two" but her frightened look said it. Had the hospital detected her pregnancy? Had she been chastised? Did her mother know? I glanced from Chastity to Ruth and then back again, deciding Chastity's secret was still safe from her parents.

"I take full responsibility," I said to her and her mother. "I have the stamina of a camel crossing the desert and a Monarch butterfly crossing the ocean. Food and drink are more for pleasure than sustenance. I can survive on air alone while spending hours and days at my typewriter. I became so engrossed in helping with the wedding, I didn't stop to eat. I'm sorry," I said to Chastity.

"You did nothing wrong, Jim." Her mother responded instead of her. "The nurse said Margie isn't the first bride-to-be to end up here exhausted from all the preparation and excitement." She resumed focusing on her daughter—on Margie. "Your father and I should have insisted you accept our help from the beginning. I just thought…well, never mind."

I suddenly realized I wasn't the elephant in the room. Dwayne was. Or his absence was.

"He will be here, Mother," Chastity said softly.

Chastity's defense of her missing fiancé sent a reminder through me of yesterday's rejection. This one stung less. Maybe because she seemed less sure. Or less concerned whether he came or not. Maybe all she had the strength for was to fend off Ruth's maternal interference and overprotection.

"I should go…" I gestured toward the waiting room.

"No." Ruth motioned for me to stay. "I will go check on Hugh. And, Margie, I mean no offense by this, but you need to decide if you are going through with…"

"I will take better care of myself, Mother. That's all I need to do."

Ruth slipped away, though I noticed a hint of motherly starch in her step. Once alone, Chastity and I gazed at each other. The elephant was no longer Dwayne, but Dwayne's baby. With or without him here, Chastity still needed one special person no other could replace in her condition—her mother. Questions, fears, and doubts I had no answers for clouded her face. If her dilemma was choosing the right sniper rifle, I was her man. But for maternal advice…

"Oh, Jim. What if…" Tears formed in her eyes. The horror of compromising this child while throwing a wedding changed the Chastity I knew into someone else. "I never thought… I didn't know, but I should have. I could have let something awful happen to…" She laid a hand below her stomach.

I stepped near her bed and laid my hand on hers. "Maybe this is…" I gave a tentative glance toward heaven. "…His way of showing you?"

Her tears glistened. "You're right. You are such a wonderful answer to prayer. My dad even said there is something good about you." She placed her free hand on

159

top of mine as color returned to her face, a glimmer of the girl I knew rising from the woman about to bear a child.

"Well, look at you." A hefty man bustled into the room, a doctor by the look of him. He took my place at Chastity's side, and I faded back. "You're looking well enough we can probably get you out of here shortly." He glanced at me. "But first, I have some poking and prodding to do, to be sure."

Panic flashed across Chastity's face, which I read like a book. Had she fooled everyone except this doctor? Was he poking and prodding and getting her alone to ferret the truth from her?

I gave Chastity a look which said, "Stiff upper lip, we will weather this," while my mouth told her doctor, "Yes, sir. I will go tell her family." Neither of them seemed buoyed by my support, so I fled the room.

Her parents weren't in the lobby where I had assumed they would be. I checked the chapel, the next logical place for a pastor and his wife, then glanced down hallways, never finding them. I returned to a practically empty lobby. "Have you seen Pastor Hugh or his wife?" I asked the receptionist, who wagged her head to indicate she hadn't. They surely wouldn't leave. I walked to the front window and scanned the parking lot where a sole, small figure walked away from the hospital. A small, brown-haired female, very casually dressed.

"Wait," I shouted at the glass. She couldn't hear and didn't turn, but every head in the vicinity did. "Sorry," I apologized to the glaring receptionist as I raced from the building. Once out front, I gazed in every direction, up and down the sidewalk, and again at the parking lot. "Hey, I-have-a-story lady," I called in case the brown-haired woman who had started my whole escapade with Chastity was anywhere nearby, but no one responded. Had I imagined her? Not just a moment ago, but from the beginning? I raked a hand through strands of hair that flopped back over my forehead, then took one more circular gaze around.

"Who are you looking for, son?"

I wheeled at the male voice and the way he said "son." Only Grandpa called me that, but it was Chastity's father who stood there.

Pastor Hugh and I locked gazes.

"We need to talk," he said. Whatever had remained unsaid earlier when he approached me in the hospital lobby had congealed into words now. And sentences. He tipped his head, indicating the length of sidewalk stretching beyond the parking lot. I joined him, the answer to prayer this pastor/father probably never had expected.

Chapter 19

Stiff as a board after her father's talk with me, I escorted Chastity to the hospital's front door.

"I feel fantastic," she boasted as I helped her into my car, which I had parked close to the entrance. She looked fantastic—even better than fantastic. "I'm surprised my parents didn't insist they drive me home, though. Aren't you?" She gave me that priceless blue-eyed look as I was about to close her door.

"Have they ever climbed that rickety ladder to your living area?" I tried to turn their absence into a joke. I knew exactly why they declined to drive her home, and it had nothing to do with her ladder.

She scrunched her face. "Once or twice," she said when I joined her inside the car, taking my place behind the steering wheel. "My decorating style never fit theirs. My bedroom as a child wasn't done in their taste, and now…" She grinned. "I suppose the ladder and my home are a little much."

I mustered a grin to match hers. Barely. The things her father had said weighed heavily on my shoulders. "I believe they wanted to drive you home, but just like accepting your decorating style, they are being good parents by putting their time and energy into what matters most to you right now. Your mother will likely be baking up a storm of cupcakes and your father drawing up the ceremony. We all have a list of things to do." I started the car. For once I told her the complete truth, yet I cringed at the falsity of it. There was more. Maybe there always was more with good parents and grandfathers.

"Hmmm," Chastity mused. "They're such kind people." She settled into her seat, a contented look on her face as we left the hospital.

She was right about her parents. But now I knew personally what a good man Pastor Hugh was. A very good man, and extremely keen. Second to my grandfather in all I found respectable and admirable.

"Actually, they are remarkable," Chastity suddenly spurted. She was right, but if she was as astute as her parents were at my behavior, she might send me straight back to New York and find herself another brides-man.

I gripped the steering wheel and drove in silence. What her father had missed, he'd explained that her mother had detected—the exceptionally healthy glow restored to Chastity's face, to her whole being. Ruth recognized what only a woman who had once carried a child could—the physiological effects of an infant in a womb.

I had cringed then like I did now. If Chastity realized that her parents knew, would she be sitting here in absolute peace? Probably not. One day wasn't nearly enough time for her and her parents to sort out how they each felt, so Hugh had asked me to help them hide their secret about knowing as well as I had helped hide the pregnancy to begin with. My face warmed at my deception, a deception Hugh took well. My agreement to keep his secret was followed by a remark that if the good guys in my books could come close to a woman's maternal detection skills, there would be no story.

"You're awfully quiet." Chastity was eyeing me, though I didn't glance her way.

"Just thinking," I responded as flippantly as I could, lost in thought about what Chastity's father had said next. The thing her mother had failed to express with care, he did by calling me "son" one last time when he finished our conversation, which ended far down the sidewalk from the hospital.

"*Son, I perceive you love my daughter.*" His words hadn't left me since he said out loud what I had failed to.

Instead of worming my way around the truth, I had looked him in the eye and admitted it. "I do, sir, I love Chastity...Margie...with all my heart."

What Hugh said next shook me to the core. "I have been looking for my daughter's fiancé. For Dwayne. He isn't where he was supposed to be. Quite honestly, I'm not surprised."

Hugh wasn't asking me to be a safety net for his daughter. I was his safety net. I saw in his eyes what he wished for from me as we waited for Dwayne to show up for the wedding. Or not show up. I couldn't tell whether Hugh thought Dwayne wouldn't arrive or if he didn't want him to. Like my grandfather, Hugh saw things he didn't divulge, because some were best learned by living them, not simply from being told.

"Are you worried about me?" Chastity set her fingers on my arm. "Is that what you are thinking about? I am fine, honestly."

I glanced to the side at her. "You always will be fine, Chastity. I will make sure of that." Right or wrong, this was my mountain and I would climb it. Even if I died in the process or reached the top alone, she had my promise. One I made with the same depth of commitment I vowed for my grandfather and Seth, that promise minus the passion she stirred in me.

"Before we get back to your house, I do need to make a couple of phone calls," I said to a look of gratitude…or maybe more…that would have at any other time stopped me dead in my tracks and restored my quandary of *She loves me* or *She loves me not*.

"Anything you need, Jim." Her face maintained an expression of…of what? Awe for my heroism. I was her hero. She recognized that. And she responded to it. This girl couldn't possibly belong to Reed's enemies. Or if she originally did, she'd just switched sides. The perfect candidate for a double spy if this were one of my novels.

"The drugstore has a telephone inside." She pointed to a building with "Grove's Pharmacy and Soda Fountain" spelled in gold letters across its large front window.

"It won't take long. I promise." My gut knotted as I pulled next to the building. I begged Heaven that my grandfather would answer his phone and Seth's secretary would tell me he had been located. *Please, God…* I checked for thugs, Clyde, Wally, or someone who might pretend to be from the *Times*. Seeing no one suspicious, I slipped inside, dashed to the phone marked for public use, and deposited enough coins to contact Seth's office.

"We haven't heard a thing." Miss Olsen dashed my hope, her voice sullen. "His wife hasn't either. Needless to say…"

Needless to say, we all feared the worst. I felt utterly empty as I hung up the phone. What could I do from here? Other than reach out to Seth's contact at the *Times*. Who may also be missing, since another man was pretending to be him.

I deposited several more coins and dialed my grandfather's number. The phone rang endlessly no matter how strenuously I willed him to answer it. He could be out—visiting a friend, at the store, or sitting in his favorite chair at the library. I swallowed loudly as I hung up and exited the drugstore. Maybe he was searching for a hotel like I told him to. Grandpa would adore Chastity, and he would find a companion of the soul in her father. Where was he?

"Is everything all right?" Chastity queried me when I climbed back into the car.

Not yet. Maybe never. "I hope so," I said and resumed our drive to her house. Though I was easy to find, and at least Clyde knew what I was driving, I passed her place on purpose, then looped back after I decided no one suspicious lurked nearby. Once parked, I eyed her ladder.

"If you are worrying about me climbing to the balcony, I can handle that," she stated. "I told you, I am fine."

"Surely there is an entrance somewhere on the lower level." I studied the ancient structure, which looked more like a hideout. "Have you been underneath the main floor?"

"The walls are surely nothing more than structure to support the upstairs."

"You're probably right," I fibbed, knowing that my fictional gangsters would choose a place exactly like this to hide their loot in. Exiting the car with all the nonchalance I could muster, I rounded it to her side and opened her door. "How did you come to live in this place?"

"It's Dwayne's. But he let me decorate it."

A thousand things I wanted to know, though I really didn't, swirled through my mind. How did they meet? Did they live here together? That would be something unheard of, for the most part, especially for a pastor's daughter.

"Well, we have a lot to do, if you are truly up for it." I took her hand and led her from the car. There had to be a stairway inside that lower level somewhere. Not to mention an exterior door to get to it. Shame on Dwayne for not making one if there wasn't. Or for not telling her if there was.

As we approached the building, I surreptitiously studied the gray, splintery boards, especially eying the thin grooves between the planks for hinges. "Ladies first," I said once we reached the ladder. If Chastity fell asleep, I would search for a trapdoor in her floor.

"That's one of the many things I like about you, Jim. You think of me. You're a good man. A very good man."

I probably blushed as I sent her up ahead of me. Rather than making her way feebly, she scaled her ladder like a squirrel, racing to the top, and smiling over the railing as I clambered up.

"If you were going to be helping me longer than one more day, I would say *you* need an easier way in, not me." Chastity laughed as I lumbered over the railing. Another day or not, I full well intended to search this building.

I unlocked her door and entered before her, checking for any sign of intrusion. Only the keenest of sleuths could be certain things were just as she left them in her kaleidoscope of colors and furniture. "Why don't you sit in my...I mean, the...pillowy chair."

She laughed at me and sank into a cushion that

swallowed her lithe form. It suited her, soft pastels encasing a head of big curls, a cute smile, and eyes that laughed.

Like a good guy, I gathered from within the kitchen some things for her to nibble on and to drink, while like a bad guy I eyed her floor for a secret way in and out. "I almost have a snack prepared. Just like the doctor ordered," I called, to which she gave no response. Leaving everything behind, I raced to where I had left her and found her in an angelic sleep, nestled deep in her chair's cushiony softness. She breathed steadily and her cheeks bore a rosy color. Dwayne was the luckiest man alive. And the stupidest for leaving her here alone with the likes of me.

I found it before she awakened. A small, almost invisible cut in the wood flooring, discreetly located in a built-in cabinet at the back. For all the open breeziness of Chastity's home, the cabinet was tight and dark. On my knees with my rump in the air, I searched with my fingers for a way to pry the trapdoor open…a vulnerable pose my characters would never risk.

I worked up a sweat, muttered words Chastity shouldn't hear, and sank more than one splinter into my fingertips looking for a trick to open it. I blamed Dwayne. What sort of man put a fiancée like Chastity in such a place as this? I grumbled and fumbled, speaking ill of whoever designed this building, until I heard my name and bolted to my feet.

"Jim?" Chastity's voice was soft, her expression sleepy and gentle when she passed through her fabric walls to where I sheepishly stood.

"Is everything all right?" I tried to erase guilt from my face.

"Someone is here asking for you." She indicated the direction of the front door.

"Clyde?" I took her by the shoulders and positioned her behind me. "A German man?"

"German?" She scrunched her face. "He didn't tell me his name, but he isn't huge like Kevin described, nor does he speak with an accent."

No matter who it was, I cringed at how easy I was to find. "Stay right where you are." I squeezed her arm to reinforce how much I wanted her to be safe. "If anything happens to me…"

Her eyes rounded.

"Never mind. Just stay here." I whisked through her billowing fabric walls until I could see the front door. No one stood there peering inside. Creeping near the window, I strained to gaze down. "Seth? Seth!" I shot through the front door and scrambled to where the ladder leaned against the balcony railing for a better look at the disheveled character standing below. It really *was* Seth. He was safe. He looked horrible, but he was alive. I wanted to giggle, I was so relieved.

"I have been looking everywhere for you." He glared, but it didn't take. Nor did I care. We were like family and both thrilled for this reunion. "What in the world are you doing up there? I mean, I understand the girl, she's a looker, but aren't you supposed to be writing? Interviewing? Sticking close to your room and a phone?" No matter how tough Seth tried to sound, his face didn't show it. But it did show exhaustion. And fear.

"Aren't you supposed to be editing?" I retorted.

His appearance terrified me. Any attempt at our usual banter was a ruse and we both knew it. Life had changed, which meant our roles had changed, along with the way we interacted.

He shuffled in Chastity's dirt yard. "That thing you said about an editor's body washing ashore on the Hudson River?"

"I didn't mean it. That was a joke."

"It isn't funny." Seth didn't look angry. In fact, I could see he didn't blame me at all. He was sincerely asking, hoping his main crime writer could finish the story so he would know how to escape his predicament safely.

"I'm sorry I ever interviewed Reed. You didn't want me to, and you were right." Now I shuffled, but on Chastity's splintery boards.

We were silent for a moment. Seth and I were used to exchanging ideas for a fictional plot, but this was real. We had no control over these bad guys, nor were we sure who they were. As Grandpa and I had concluded, at least one of us knew the bad guy. We just didn't realize he was bad.

"It doesn't look to me like you've been suffering as much as I have." Seth snorted as he jerked his head toward the door behind me.

"She's engaged," I hissed over the rail. "It's not what you think."

He snorted again, then dismissed his attempt at normalcy with a wave of his hand. "Never mind that. We need to talk."

This was the second time today a man said that to me. Though likely a different topic, I couldn't imagine my conversation with Seth would be any lighter than the one I'd had with Chastity's father.

"Chastity," I called inside to her. "I will be right back. It's my editor. He looks rough, but he isn't a bad guy, meaning he isn't the villainous type. He's not really a good guy, either." I flung a leg over the railing and worked my way down the ladder to the ground.

"Chastity?" Seth whispered, gazing up to the balcony.

"That's what she calls herself."

Seth snorted again. Then coughed to cover it up when I took a step closer.

"Sorry," he muttered for probably the first time in his life. "Look, Jim. I know you came here because you truly do have the right to a life outside of writing…" Another first for Seth, but I said nothing so he would say what neither of us wanted to hear. "But your life is in danger. So is mine. And I expect others besides Reed are possible targets. We need to go somewhere safe."

I gulped. Then looked up because Seth did. Chastity's angelic face peered down at us as she rested her elbows on the railing.

"I won't leave here until I am sure she is safe," I whispered as I waved at her. "I'm not quite sure how to do that, since Reed as well as Clyde…who is his own kind of terrifying, by the way…both said I am easy to find. Heck, you found me and you have no skills whatsoever in detection. So it's easy to assume both criminal elements know I am here, which puts her in danger even if I leave." Not to mention that the elusive Dwayne no one seemed to have a handle on or complete confidence in might not make her safety a priority.

"Take her with you." Seth shrugged.

"I can't do that. She is getting married tomorrow." Or could I? I looked again at the face that changed my whole world. She would be better off with me. I would never leave her in a dump like this place. Chastity didn't love me, though. She loved Dwayne. I had achieved nothing more than hero status with her.

I turned back to Seth. "I'm staying here."

"You can't do that." His voice hit a note I never knew possible for a man. "You have an obligation. The publisher needs you, your fans need you, those who read the *Times* need you." Desperation caused him to grasp at straws that under the circumstances paled in significance. "Your grandfather also needs you," he added the crown to his list of reasons. The one which truly mattered.

"Grandpa. How is he? Do you know?"

"He had a little bout of something right before I figured out I was being followed. As much as he frightens me, I made sure he got some medical attention. He and I are oil and water, but he works on a person. Like you do. That's the last time I saw him. When I got a couple of threatening notes, I took off."

I wanted to hug and choke Seth at the same time. Maybe just a hug since that sort of sign of affection would be too much for him. "Who was following you? What did the notes say? Did whoever-it-was see you with Grandpa?" I didn't know whether to wring his hand or his neck.

"Slow down. I never saw who was following me. It was one of those creepy sensations of being watched. When the notes came, I knew I was right." Seth stretched and shoved a hand into his pocket, extracting two grimy and soiled folds of paper, which he shoved at me.

Horrified by what they probably were, I trembled as I opened them and shook when I read them. "These are my words," I gasped and looked at Seth. "But I didn't write these notes, just the words."

Seth swiped them from my hand and stuffed them back into his pocket. A tough move, but there was nothing tough in his expression. "I know you didn't write or send these to me. But whoever did write them has read your books. I recognized the threats from a couple of your stories." The look he'd had earlier, the one after he reminded me of my remark about an editor's body washing ashore on the Hudson River, returned. Suddenly I was more than his golden boy in fictional storytelling— I was his golden prophet, as if whatever I wrote would happen.

"It doesn't work like that, Seth," I addressed his desperate look. "I'm not writing fact. Someone is taking my fiction and turning it *into* fact."

"Close enough." He slapped the pocket with the warning notes. "Whoever did this probably read the ending of your book and won't be foolish enough to get caught in the same way, but they are making a point."

We shuffled awkwardly in Chastity's dirt yard, seeking out new bearings for tense discussions without a desk between us. I pondered the two books those notes had been taken from. In one the criminal was a crooked cop, the other a soured bank vice president. Succumbing to temptation was the downfall of the first, and revenge for a failed career motivated the second. The intended connection to Seth and me might be the cop's written threat to a possible snitch to keep quiet. The quote from the angry VP was an intentional false lead he planted, a kind statement about the one he held a grudge against.

I raked a hand through my hair. "Honestly, Seth, I'm not sure the quotes themselves mean anything. I think it has more to do with the fact they are familiar to both of us. That makes it personal." And creepy.

"And narrows the list of suspects to only those who have read your books." He snorted again, but barely. "That would be most of America."

I had forgotten about Chastity and glanced up. There she stood, just as before, leaning on the banister railing and gazing down at us with her beautiful face surrounded by a halo of yellow curls, more yellow than ever with the sun highlighting them. She waved at me with her fingers. She had read my books. At least she claimed she had. But she didn't know Seth. At least not directly, or enough to orchestrate a warning to him. I raked my fingers through my hair again.

"You know someone is impersonating your contact at the *Times*?" I shifted my gaze and the direction of my conversation to Seth.

He nodded. "I don't know what can of worms you opened by interviewing Reed, but those worms are nasty. I can't even talk to my wife for fear they will go after her. She went to stay with my mother, something so unthinkable no one will look for her there." Seth glanced around. "I would guess you're right that you are easy to find. So maybe this isn't the best place for us to be standing."

Seth would faint if I took him up to Chastity's world of delight. I glanced around, knowing I couldn't suddenly identify a safe place in this part of Grove. Or anywhere in Grove, for that matter.

"Look, Jim. We know the ropes in New York. We understand that city. We know nothing about a tiny place like this. We should go back. We'll still have to watch our backs, but we know our way around there." Seth was desperate. Suddenly I realized he hadn't come here to hide and save himself; he had come for me. Shortly after making sure Grandpa was taken care of. The one person I longed most to see but knew I couldn't. And wouldn't until this was all settled, for his sake.

A lemony scent overwhelmed me, and a soft hand intertwined with mine before I could say yes or no to Seth's plea.

"You should go, Jim." Chastity's voice sounded worried.

Only a rogue would leave this girl behind. A rogue like Dwayne. "You have a wedding coming up and I am your brides-man."

"You're what?" Seth sputtered.

"Jim is being modest. Actually, he is more a Man of Honor." Chastity smiled. Only for a moment, then her face sobered. "But not now. I am releasing you from that obligation, Jim. Go wherever you have to go to be safe."

Even if her father hadn't called me "son" and given me the charge of watching for Dwayne, I would never go.

"I won't leave you," I informed her. Until Chastity said "I do" to Dwayne...if he showed up. After that, I would be gone.

"But..." She looked truly worried, not at all like a conniving person who would copy threatening quotes from two of my books.

I did what I had wanted to do since I met her. I touched her lips. Not with mine, as I preferred, but with a finger to hush her protest. "I am staying. That's that. I promised you I would stay until everything is ready."

A finger that smelled like lemons touched my lips. "Maybe it's the bride-to-be in me," she said, her lips warm against my finger. "But I will never leave you or forsake you, either. I am with you until death do us part."

175

I didn't just hear vows, I felt them. In the air, caught up by angels maybe. All I had to do was say the same and we would be bound. Was marriage more of a heavenly act than a human one? The solemnity of her promise showed in her eyes.

"I love you for all you do for me, Jim Turner." She took both my hands, and we faced each other.

Seth cleared his throat. I had forgotten all about him. When I turned, he almost smiled. "I see you still have a way with words, Turner. Just not the kind I pay you for."

"Actually, my grandfather has a way with words." He spoke them, and he lived them, but he never wrote them. Seth wouldn't like it, but maybe it was time for me to stop writing about blood and write with it.

I pulled Chastity close and held her against me, this embrace being one of those fleeting moments of eternity that lasted forever, according to my grandfather.

Drowning myself in lemon, yellow, pastels, and a lithe form that fit mine exactly, for these few seconds I understood what the expression "Heaven on Earth" truly meant.

Chapter 20

I kept Seth outside with me while Chastity returned to her colorful abode, an ethereal delight I didn't think he could handle in his weakened condition. Or any other time, for that matter.

"Someday I would love to know what in the world happened to you here," he said once Chastity disappeared through her door. He eyed the pastel fabric the breeze caught and exposed through the openings. "But not now. It scares me more than your grandfather does, frankly, but we have other frightening situations to contend with."

I nodded in agreement, spotted what must have been his car parked out front, and headed toward it. Seth followed, and soon we were sequestered inside where no one should be able to hear us.

"You're still the same Jim Turner I knew in New York, aren't you?" He scrutinized me.

"That and more," I assured him.

"The 'more' shows all over you."

I wanted to smile. "I will try to contain it until we get through this."

What Seth saw as a weakness, a chink in our armor that might get both of us killed, I realized was a strength. Love was powerful. It raised up heroes. It motivated and fought to the death. No wonder Grandpa sent me here. What I'd learned not only made me a better writer, it made me a better man.

"I never thought I would get any closer to the criminal element than I did plotting your stories. This is real and I admit I'm at a bit of a loss." His weary expression pinched with more lines. He needed sleep, he needed food, he needed Grandpa's peninsula. But at this point, the shock of the peninsula might kill him.

"I'm at a loss myself," I confessed. "We know Reed is dead and someone is impersonating your contact at the *Times*. A large woman told me I am being watched, and I was, at least by a hotel clerk named Wally. Then there is Clyde. He found me. Besides getting away from him intact, I came away knowing he was aware of Reed. He said Reed had a big mouth. He also said you and I were both easy to find."

Seth paled more than he already was. I probably did too as we sat in his car pondering our dilemma.

"Where is the article you wrote from Reed's interview?"

I ran a hand under my shirt and extracted it from the leather pouch against my chest. It and my story. I handed him the article only. "I rewrote it," I said. "Reed would have been killed sooner if I printed what he said. This one is what the situation is really about."

I knew Seth would explode when he read the love story that had deserved to be written. I braced myself and sat quietly watching his face change colors as he took in every word.

"You're kidding," he said at last. He looked up from the pages. "The *Times* won't print this."

"I don't intend for them to. They will never see it."

"Then why did you write it?" Red began creeping up Seth's neck.

"For the deserter. It's his story, and I think it's the truth."

Seth burst into laughter. "When were you going to ask him to read it? When the two of you met for coffee somewhere?"

"Possibly right before he kills me."

Seth sobered. "You won't get that chance. You will never see him coming."

"Because he will take me like a sniper? I have already thought of that. That's why I'm carrying it on me."

Seth toyed with the steering wheel. "From what you wrote about him, he might not be the one doing the killing. He's in love. He has two people to protect because she is counting on him."

"How would you know a thing like that?" This was a man whose world view was from a second-floor window. The rest of his life was taken from fictional stories, mine in particular.

"I'm deducing. We know that whoever wants Reed's story destroyed, he wants it bad."

"Badly," I corrected my editor.

Seth rolled his eyes. "Anyway, my contact had information on whoever killed Reed, before he and I lost communication. The physical description didn't fit what we know of the deserter."

"Who did it fit?" I asked.

"You, sort of."

If my hair ever did anything other than lie flat over my forehead, it would have stood straight on end at that moment. My scalp tingled and my skin went cold. "Me? They think I killed Reed? This is worse than using quotes from my books."

"Don't worry. I defended you."

"But now you're in hiding. Which makes both of us look guilty. Who in the world thought they saw me shooting someone?"

"A nobody. Some hotel clerk around here. That's why I came to Grove…besides hiding out myself, I hoped to get you to safety."

My mind spun. Wally? Kevin? Everything I knew about them whirled in my head until at last Wally shook loose. "The clerk's name is Wally," I stated with conviction. "He was posing as a hotel clerk, but I always knew something was off about him. He probably shot Reed himself and made up the story about me." I tightened my fists. He was probably the one who ransacked my room, since he had access to a key. "His only saving grace when it comes to your warning notes is that I doubt he read a word of my books. Just memorized the titles and main characters."

"He merely described someone like you. A pretty clever way to pin a bigger target on you to anyone who wanted to put a stop to this story." Seth dropped back against the driver's door and rested his head on the window. He looked even more exhausted than he had an hour ago.

"So what do we do?"

At that point Chastity stepped onto her balcony. I couldn't see her, since my back was to her house, but I saw her in Seth's expression. That's what her sort of beauty did to a man. It made him vulnerable. Distracted him enough he would forget his focus. As we both repositioned to watch her lithe strides along the balcony, we became easy targets. Sitting ducks. A dead duck in my case, since all that had been important to me meant nothing compared to keeping my promise to her.

"Watch that one," Seth said from behind me.

"I am."

"I mean *watch out*. Because of her."

As glad as I was to have Seth back, if we were in his office right now, I would shove him through the window's glass for his suspicious insinuation regarding her character. But I resisted doing or saying anything rash to the man I needed and who needed me, by keeping my focus on her. She stopped her pacing and looked our way. Not at me, though. Those large blue eyes studied Seth the same way his did her.

"She's a pastor's daughter," I said in her defense. "Keep in mind, she's getting married tomorrow. That is all that matters to her right now."

"Not really."

I wheeled around and faced Seth.

"You want to marry her. And I would lay odds she feels the same about you." Maybe it was his glasses, and his curly hair and slight pudginess, that gave him a look of innocent sincerity. But I knew better. This was my editor. The one who did everything he could to keep me all to himself. Seth had no discernment, no inner intuitiveness, and no heart. He operated to make money only, and I was his bread and butter. "I have never seen you in love before, Jim. I always dreaded it, knowing someday those soulish things your grandfather said could taint your keen edge."

"I do want to marry her." It came out in a whoosh. But it felt good. Like a confession of love that needed released. "If I could, I would."

"Where is her fiancé? Not many would tolerate some other man longing for their intended."

"He's gone. That's all I know. But he's supposed to be here tomorrow in time for the wedding."

"Then he isn't that far away," Seth said with surprising astuteness.

My skin chilled, even in the warmth of his car. Dwayne was close? He certainly could be. Something else Pastor Hugh had said to me that I had dismissed as simple parental protectiveness came back: *We aren't sure about him, but I am about you.*

"Excuse me." I started to climb out of Seth's car. Risking my life was one thing, but risking Chastity's was another. She needed to know everything, while she had a choice. It was too late for me.

"Wait." Seth grabbed my arm. With my car door half open, I looked back at him. "I have a plan. And before you involve her, you need to hear it."

Seth had a plan? Desperate times truly brought out the best in him. I closed my door and faced him fully. "Will I like it?"

"The part of you that is related to your grandfather will." Seth truly was a changed man.

"Go on."

He hadn't read my story, but he kept my version of Reed's, which he tapped with a finger. "We are going to publish this."

My mouth dropped open. I was speechless. Completely wordless, for once.

"Instead of to the *Times*, I say we give it to Chicago's paper. It's big, with a wide circulation. If it goes AP, that will do it. Everyone who doesn't want Reed's story published will see yours. It's a risk. A huge one. But you wrote the story of a hero. The deserter will have a chance to see it before you're in his crosshairs…hopefully…and change his mind. Maybe. The article will still rile someone, but if my idea works, it won't be him." Seth finished and waited. "You can close your mouth now, Jim."

It was almost impossible to shut my mouth while filled with so much awe. My mind whirled with amazement at Seth, the incredulity of his plan, the life-and-death brink he set me on. Which made me wonder. If I was gone, truly and finally gone, would that matter to Chastity? If Seth's intuition was right, and she meant what she'd said earlier, it would. Because I did.

I reached for my car door's handle.

"Wait." Seth stopped me. "What's your answer, first?"

I looked from him to the blonde girl I would live and die for. "Publish it," I said. At his relieved but foreboding look, I stepped from his car and walked to beneath where Chastity stood.

"We need to talk," I said the same way her father and Seth had both said it to me. She beckoned me up, but I refused. I needed absolute clarity when I told her all she needed to know, something I lacked when in her colorful abode.

Chapter 21

I stared into a face I had trusted and wanted to continue trusting.

Chastity stood in front of me, the breeze arranging and rearranging her large yellow curls around her head. "What is it, Jim?"

I could feel Seth's gaze at my back, strangely supportive since he and I both were on unfamiliar ground. He lacked the knack for ferreting out the sinister and knew nothing about the female mind, yet here I was, trusting his plan regarding a deadly enemy, and bordering on operating on his earlier advice of "Take her with you."

"Before I talk to you about what is really on my mind, you should know more about me."

She gave me a soft laugh. "I know everything about you, Jim Turner. I told you that when we first met."

My grand confessions and professions stuttered at the reminder. She was right. More than once, Chastity had proclaimed she knew everything there was to know.

"You successfully write crime novels, plus you write articles for the *Times*. You have never been married or even close to it, the person most important to you is your grandfather. You have a hero's heart, though maybe not his courage…yet. But you will. Your ties to the current war are like a safe flirtation—you are intrigued and willing, but not sure you will fit in. You also have a poet's heart in a practical mind and body. Is that enough, or do you want me to continue?"

I felt naked in front of her big blue eyes for the second time. "You left out how much I hate Dwayne." Chastity had effectively covered my past and present, so it was time to speak of my future. At least of the one I wanted.

Her eyes widened and then clouded. She looked away.

If Seth was right that Dwayne was probably close by, he could walk up on Chastity and me at any moment. He could be watching from somewhere near enough to see an exchange no fiancé would want his intended engaged in.

"If I said I'm sorry, it would only mean I am sorry that it's true. But that won't keep me from doing everything I can to make sure you are happy and marry the man you love."

She was right when she detected my hero's heart. Meeting her while learning from Grandpa and the deserter brought that out in me. But the courage she said would also come appeared now. Not in a willingness to engage Dwayne in a duel for her hand, but in the strength it took to lay down all I wanted for the sake of her happiness.

When she finally looked at me, her eyes were watery, her cheeks faintly pink, and her expression one of a woman under so much pressure her glitter had lost its sparkle. "Promise?" she asked, her voice barely a whisper. "Promise me you will do that."

My dark side responded on the inside with an adamant, "Never, not in a thousand years," while I, the Jim Turner this woman certainly knew well and engaged as her answer to prayer, said out loud, "Yes. I promise."

"Thank you. I will hold you to it." She tried to smile, but like her voice, it was weak. "Now," she straightened a bit, "was there more you wanted to talk about?"

While my dark side listed the various reasons I should retract my promise, I held strong to my vow. "I'm in a bit of a sticky situation. Seth is also." I indicated my editor still sitting in his car, his gaze fixed on us as we talked.

I studied her as she studied Seth. The first day I met Chastity, I concluded she lived in a happy bubble, willingly and blissfully ignorant of the world around her, even with a world war brewing. But something keener eyed my editor. Something knowledgeable that was fully aware of life's darker side. Chastity suddenly seemed a beautifully wrapped package of cunning and wisdom I hadn't expected to find.

"I thought so," she finally said and turned her gaze upon me. "You would never leave or have left my side unless something else was going on. Just like Dwayne." With that she turned and climbed her ladder the faltering way I usually did instead of like a happy squirrel.

I wheeled to look at Seth whose shrug and raised hands showed him to be as baffled as I was. My good and not-so-good inner voices struck up a war inside me. "She is hurting," one said, while the other chided, "She knows something."

I raced to Seth's car and leaned inside. His recent scares had changed him, but I didn't expect any sound advice on his part about love and women.

"I have to go talk to her," I informed him. "And you can't stay out here alone, so, brace yourself, you're coming with me." I expected Seth to struggle even more than I did the first time I climbed Chastity's ladder into her abode of sensual delight, but his slight frown of skepticism was worry for me, not for himself.

"Be careful on the ladder," I warned him. Needlessly, since my slightly pudgy editor scampered right up it, shocking and annoying me. Once we were both on the balcony, I pondered whether or not to brace him for the delightful interior he was about to step into.

"What's that smell?" Seth crinkled his nose. "Lemons?"

"Come on." I waved him to follow me. Somehow it felt wrong to bring him into the sanctuary where I had lived my best life. He was my past, and my past didn't belong in this wonderful present, so I gauged him closely as we entered her home.

"Whoa," he said with a low voice as we passed through her doorway. "Look at all of this." Seth froze where he stood, moving only his head as he took in Chastity's otherworldly realm of color and scent, fluid walls, tasteful clutter, and cloud-like furniture.

I was jealous. Afraid. Felt ridiculous and defensive all at the same time. I shouldn't have brought the past me into the world of the new me. If he said one word against her...

Instead of a verbal comment, Seth let out a low whistle. "I wish you had never come to Grove," he said at last.

I relaxed the fists I'd made. The tautness drained from my stance. If I hadn't come to Grove, I would never have experienced or known the parts of a man's heart Grandpa wanted to show me. I would have continued to write about crime instead of facing it. I would have remained at my grandfather's side instead of being in the thick of his story.

"Parts of me came to Grove to die and other parts to live." What I said sounded like something Grandpa would say. The sort of lofty statement Seth normally would have brushed aside, but this time he didn't.

"I never thought I would say something like this, but you should write this down."

I patted my chest where the leather pouch hid the deserter's story, which included Grandpa's and mine. "I already have. If…I mean when…we make it out of this, I will let you read it."

Seth gazed where I placed my hand and gave me a look stripped of his usual cold view of life. This was a kinder Seth, who I prayed would not only stay alive but stay exactly like this for the rest of his years. "Go talk to her," he said. "I'll wait here." Contentedly, apparently, since he gazed at Chastity's realm of color in childlike awe.

"Don't move. And don't touch anything," I said to a side of Seth I didn't know how to control. And neither would he. Knowing he didn't register my commands, I hurried to the depths of Chastity's home, threading my way through drapes of color, calling her name as I wove around each fabric wall.

She didn't answer. Alarm spiked up. I had hurt her. Evidently another resemblance to Dwayne. I inwardly admonished myself for once again snuffing her light. "Chastity?" I called outside the fabric wall I assumed blocked the way to her bedroom. Still no response. No sound of crying, either. Daring to draw the fabric aside, I lost my breath at what I saw…no, beheld…on the other side. This was no ordinary bedroom. People wouldn't sleep in here; they would live in comatose dreams…euphorically float through the night in a womb of pastels, aromas, and textures. I let out a low whistle. This room was utter bliss. Add Chastity to it, and…

"Stop it," I barked out loud.

"Everything all right?" Seth called from the entry area, his voice minus its usual edge. He too had been affected by Chastity's world.

"Fine." I wrangled some self-control. "I haven't found her yet, but I'm still looking."

"No hurry. I'm good here." So unlike the Seth I knew.

It took every ounce of my new heroic strength to tear myself away from where Chastity slept. I inhaled the delicate aroma, noted the various candles, angular draping of swaths of fabric, pillows galore of all sizes, and the yellow table beside her bed. So much like the yellow envelope Grandpa always had waiting for me on bedside tables in my hotels. He would love this, her whole house, and her. As I imagined him standing here beside me, taking in everything I saw and felt, a glint of gold caught my eye. A gold pen lying next to a small book on top the yellow table. Chastity wrote? Stories? Poems? A diary? With a gold pen?

"Go look at it," my dark inner voice urged. "I'm telling you, she can't be trusted."

To my surprise, my good voice said almost the same thing. "Go look at it. You will understand her better."

"No," I said to both, though the draw to whatever she wrote was the most powerful force I had ever encountered. "No," I said again with less conviction, and I took a step back. After a moment, I let the cloth wall I had been holding fall into place, blocking my view of heaven as I imagined it. And whatever it was Chastity had to say. And wrote about.

I kept moving backward, more like staggering, my gaze glued to the thin material that kept me from all I wanted. What if Chastity caught me in there? Reading her thoughts, no less. I wouldn't take that chance. I wouldn't destroy whatever trust she might still have in me.

I continued to back away. My heel caught on something, and I lost my balance. With only drapes of fabric to grab onto, I let myself free fall to the splintery floor. The back of my head landed solidly. It hit hard enough I lay stunned, the colors above me meshing into a dizzying swirl interrupted by a fuzzy head and round glasses.

"Jim, you all right?"

I focused. Seth. I batted my eyes, slowing the circulating room until I could distinguish his features. "I guess so." I raised an arm and felt the back of my head. "Ouch. I guess I tripped and fell." I tried to raise myself to my elbows, but the dizzying sensation returned.

"Lie still, buddy."

Buddy? Had I been knocked unconscious?

I remained flat on the floor and watched Seth take in the area where I lay. "Yep, you tripped all right." He peered near my feet. "Some kind of wood." He bent closer. "It looks like a trap door that's been pulled open."

At that I jolted up, grabbing my head in the process, biting against the pain, and pressing my eyes shut to stop the incessant swirling. When at last both abated a bit, I opened one eye and looked where Seth now squatted, straddling one of my legs.

"Right here." He tapped on the piece of wood I had unsuccessfully been able to move earlier while searching for a trap door. It lay shoved to the side of a hole in the floor. A square hole where Chastity had apparently gone.

I didn't know if the tears that blurred what I saw were from the head pain or from the agony which seized my heart. Chastity had known all along how to get to the lower level of this building and evidently away from it. She had lied. Possibly used me, but why? To make use of my writing skills didn't seem reason enough.

I lay back on the floor and kept my eyes closed to keep my tears in and what I could see of Chastity's home out. Seth surprisingly and kindly said nothing as he settled on the floor and waited.

Chapter 22

I ached from head to toe, inside and out, as I lay on Chastity's splintery floor, shamed that a term such as "irony" had escaped me as an author, the unworn floor shouting that no one really lived here. This building was a stage set for a fool to believe in, the starring actress an untold beauty, an antagonist disguised as a heroine in need.

Leaving me as no hero at all, for her motive was nefarious, a tie to Reed or those who took him out. I was merely a stooge who happened by, a pawn in this supposed love story.

"I was played as a fool," I moaned, covering my face with my hands. "No, I played a fool." I would have sobbed if I weren't so furious…and in Seth's view. Who was still strangely quiet. I parted two fingers and peered through them.

If the statue of the thinker wore glasses and had a slightly round face, Seth could have been him as he struck a pensive pose. He shifted slightly and rubbed his chin as if in deep thought. "Could be," he finally drawled.

"No, there is no doubt. I made classic mistakes. The kind that get a good man gunned down." Fury and humiliation maimed Jim Turner the writer, but a bullet through the heart just took Jim Turner of Mountain Grove down. I hurt. This must have been the moment my grandfather told me about. Writing life on the page from a heart so torn by loving someone that my blood became the ink.

I lay there in misery, realizing yet once more the story I had been writing was inadequate. Even though I wrote with Grandpa's gold pen, I had yet to write from this depth, with this much agony. Maybe, like Grandpa, I would stop short of writing the pain that no words could describe. And our family gold pen would...

"Seth." I bolted to my elbows, searing pain arcing through my head.

"Hold on there, buddy."

Buddy again? Maybe Seth had bumped his head. Or maybe Grove was to blame in both of our cases.

"Lie back down." With an uncharacteristic touch of his hands, he gently pressed against my shoulders until I lay back on Chastity's floor, which felt like a bed of nails.

The room swirled above me, but the image of her gold pen and the book she had been writing in didn't budge as I recalled them. The image was so vivid, I reached up to touch them, then retracted my hand. No. Reading her words would be wrong. But I should. I had to. Maybe my life and Seth's depended on what she might have divulged, no matter how much it further shattered everything I felt for her.

"Help me up," I groaned, struggling to my elbows again.

Seth, who never had a soul that I knew of, was unbelievably dedicated. He didn't argue, but with great care helped me to a sitting position.

"You're not thinking about crawling into that hole through the floor, are you?" he queried.

"No, I'm going to let you do that. Help me all the way up. There is something else I need to do." It wasn't easy getting me to my feet, nor was standing without toppling over. Nausea rose from within, fueled by disorientation, the bump on my head, and the utter devastation of my heart. If I lived through this moment, I didn't care if I died at some point afterward. What was there to live for? Even if I wrote this story, who would believe it? My status as a renowned author of crime would be destroyed.

"Help me get to what was...or was meant to seem like...Chastity's bedroom. There is something there I need to look at."

Seth compliantly positioned himself at my side and held me steady as I wove toward her room. My inner voices were out of control in my head, a mixture of hallelujahs and dire warnings so meshed together I didn't know which opinions belonged to which. Good or bad, right or wrong, Chastity's book might be my only chance to learn the truth.

Once we staggered through the cloth opening to her room, we both stopped. Seth let out another low whistle, taking in a marvel of sensuality he and I had both missed in our lives. How did Chastity do that? How did her essence ooze seduction while she bore a name and behavior...at least toward me...of absolute purity?

I shook off my wonder. It was all an act, and I fell for it. "That book over there on the yellow nightstand. Can you get it for me?"

Making sure I was stable against a vertical board, Seth made his way around Chastity's bed, careful not to touch it. I didn't blame him. Once at the nightstand, he gingerly lifted the book.

"Get the pen too," I said, knowing it was wrong. Gold pens were personal, sacred, the bearers of blood and truth. I wavered as Seth lifted it from the nightstand with two fingers. He too evidently sensed its hallowedness. If I didn't need both hands to hold me up, I would smack my forehead. I was getting carried away. Must be from the fall I took.

Once Chastity's book and pen lay in my hand, nothing in me could read what she had written. "We will look at this later," I said with as much command as I could fake. "Let's check out the trap door first."

I could hear the creak of wood along with a series of grunts as Seth maneuvered his slight pudginess through the hole and worked his way down a ladder.

"It's dark down here," he said once his groans and the ladder's ceased.

Candles. I should have thought of that. "Hold on." Not letting go of Chastity's book or gold pen, I maintained my balance with my other hand as I returned to her bedroom. It felt like desecrating a shrine as I removed a candle from her room. In the kitchen I found matches, and with the ease of a blind man, I stumbled back to the trapdoor opening where Seth's head and shoulders now jutted up.

Holding the candle, I struck a match and lit it. He and the wavering flicker disappeared into the dark space, a soft glow illuminating the area below once he stepped from the last rung.

"What do you see?" I knew better than to tip forward and hang my head through the opening once I settled at the hole's edge on my knees. Seth's face took on eerie shadowing as he pivoted and looked around.

"Not much yet." He and the glow moved away,

leaving me with only my imagination as the sound of cautious footsteps rose from the hole.

"Who owns this house?" Seth's voice floated up at me.

"Her fiancé, Dwayne. Why?"

"He's either loaded or a thief. This place is lined with finer furnishings than I will ever own."

With my free hand, I gripped the wood at the opening's edge. If those belonged to Dwayne, why weren't they in the upper level where Chastity lived? "Are they Chastity's type of furniture?" I hollered down to Seth.

"No, not at all. These are more fitting to royalty. Well, that's an exaggeration, but you know what I mean. These things weren't cheap." Seth and his glowing candle returned to the ladder's base. "She clearly knew this stuff was here, since she must have gone out this way."

Which meant there was a door somewhere to the outside down there. Not one merely large enough for her, but sizeable enough for furniture to pass through it. "Do you mind looking for a door of some sort?" I asked. "I'm sorry. I wish I could help."

"No problem," Seth replied, another anomaly as far as who he was and had always been.

I watched the tiny glow disappear, then relied on my ears as I heard tapping on wood around the area below.

"Found it," he said at last. A series of grunts and frustrated huffs followed as he evidently checked for a way to open the door. Suddenly light flooded what I could see at the base of the ladder, a jubilant shout from Seth coming at the same time. "It was tricky, but opening it was easy once I found the catch." His smiling face appeared below me, a snuffed candle in his hand.

"I'm coming down," I said. Nothing could stop me. Not my aching head, the spinning room, or Seth's worried frown. With Chastity's book and pen pinned to my side, I basically toppled down the ladder, hitting the ground with another thud, my buttocks suffering this time. From my sitting position on the floor, I gazed...gaped...around the area in awe. "Is that velvet?" I squinted at ornate chairs and a sofa along one wall.

"Red velvet," Seth clarified. "Really nice stuff."

I didn't ask for help as I clambered to my feet, using the ladder as a brace. But I did ask for support as I teetered toward the furniture. Seth lent himself to me as a human crutch, the two of us ambling to and then along the finest furnishings I had ever seen.

"Who is this Dwayne guy?" I asked once we had seen it all.

Seth cleared his throat.

"What?" I frowned down at him.

"Have you ever seen Dwayne?" Seth extracted himself from my armpit.

"No. He's been away."

"Then we know nothing about him. Or if he's even real. Or who he supposedly is. Which means..." At Seth's pause I looked back at fixtures that contradicted the girl who lived above them.

I groaned. My heart ached more, a self-preserving flame of anger rising with it. "All of this could well be hers." Which furthered her pretense. I sagged at the thought and Seth was quick to prop me up again.

"Let's get out of here," he said, and he steered me toward the hole of light—a huge sliding door. Even if I had had the chance to search for a doorway from the outside, I never would have thought to look for something this size. I would have missed it completely.

"I fell for all of it," I muttered as we stepped into daylight. Other than glancing down from Chastity's back balcony once, I had never seen her back yard. Which was as ghastly as the front, clods and patches of dirt interrupted by the occasional weed. "Whoever owns that furniture has no investment in this place at all."

Seth left me drooping in misery as he did his best to close the door. Once it was sufficiently shut, he rested my armpit on his shoulder again and walked me to the front yard. "We need to get you checked out at a hospital," he said.

I was too miserable to argue. I was also too miserable to live, though the crime writer in me knew fear might be a more appropriate emotion. I let Seth drag me to his car and settle me into its seat. While he drove us to the hospital, I worked to hide Chastity's book, which was thankfully small, and her gold pen in the pouch hidden beneath my shirt. If I ever wrote a crime novel again, all my good guys would wear hidden bags like this.

"The stuff under Chastity's house could be stolen," Seth offered as I leaned against the passenger door.

I considered what he said, looking for any ray of hope in it. "Since she had to know it was there, that only adds to her crimes." Her main crime being the way she had deceived me. My misery magnified as I realized those fixtures could well be Dwayne's gifts to Chastity. All I had to offer her was a story. My story. With a pen the same color as the one she likely wrote my dismissal with.

Once at the hospital, I was ushered quickly to a room

where the doctor likely surmised my condition to be far worse than it was, since a broken heart made me act nearly comatose. Seth did all the talking while I sat on the edge of the examining bed, my head hanging down. We probably looked like a guilty couple of liars, Seth disheveled and in need of a bath, while I didn't bother to make eye contact or conversation.

I only looked up when a woman's voice said, "Hey, weren't you in here recently with Pastor Hugh's family?" I jerked my head up so quickly, I yelped.

Pastor Hugh and his wife Ruth. And Margie. Were they all three phonies? Or were her parents also duped by Chastity's ruse?

"You know him well?" I asked, squinting as the doctor examined the knot on the back of my head.

"Everyone knows Pastor Hugh." She smiled and sailed around the bed, gathering whatever they would need to make me feel better. At least on the outside. "He's a saint."

I wanted to snort that his daughter certainly wasn't one, but it would hurt too much. "He seems nice." It was all I could muster.

"A lot of people around here owe him a lot. Good man. No, he's a great man. A good friend to have. You are fortunate." She patted my knee with a smile and left the room in a whoosh.

While the doctor decided I hadn't suffered a concussion and prescribed a day or two of taking it easy, I pondered Pastor Hugh, who must have been duped by his daughter since his concern was Dwayne's reliability, not hers.

Several dollars later, Seth assisted me to his car, where we sat silently in the hospital's parking lot. I leaned my head against the window and explained what I knew about Chastity's parents and their stellar reputations.

"What next?" Seth strummed his fingers on the steering wheel.

"Let's get my car," I muttered, raising a hand against Seth's immediate protest at my driving. "I'm only moving it to my first hotel's parking lot. That will confuse anyone looking for me. I will ride with you to my new hotel where we will both clean up and get something to eat."

"And rest," he added.

"We have three things we need to tend to. I want to call Grandpa again. And I agree with you that we need to take my rendition of Reed's article to the Chicago newspaper. Then…" I patted my chest where my hidden pouch lay. "I need to look at Chastity's book."

With a nod of agreement, Seth started his car and headed toward Chastity's house. I rode in silence, never removing my hand from where my story and hers lay.

Chapter 23

With my car parked at my first hotel, Seth and I headed out of Grove and stopped at an obscure phone booth outside of a small grocer where we each made calls. Grandpa still didn't answer his phone, so I sat and fretted over where he might be while Seth informed his wife and Miss Olsen that he was fine and with me. I thought I heard a low "I love you" whispered into the phone before he hung up from talking to his wife. I wondered if she lay unconscious on his mother's living room floor at hearing three words Seth had likely been stingy with during their marriage.

Though Chastity's betrayal burned a hole in my heart, Grandpa's safety and whereabouts filled my mind. I paced, pondered, and worried while Seth and I cleaned up at my new hotel room, and then we went for something to eat.

"Who is your grandfather's best friend?" the old familiar Seth asked around a mouthful of fried steak lathered in gravy.

"Me, of course." I picked at a tuna fish sandwich.

"Besides you. Does he have a girlfriend? Someone he plays checkers with?" Thankfully Seth wiped his mouth with a napkin between bites.

"When's the last time you ate? You act half starved." I frowned at his wolfish scarfing of his food.

"The moment I got the first threat," he replied

pensively. "Yep, the meal before that was the last time I ate."

Utterly ashamed at nitpicking at a man who had done nothing but good for me at such a great sacrifice to his own wellbeing, I shoved my plate in front of him. "Eat up. I can live on nothing."

"You look like it, too." He reached for my sandwich and raked it through the gravy on his plate before taking a huge bite.

I glanced around for a pay phone while Seth tore into our food like a hungry lion. "You're right," I said to him after spotting one near the café's exit. "Grandpa has friends and places he goes. I will call around until I find him. Order more food if you want." I rose as Seth waved our waitress over.

"Please be safe somewhere," I muttered to myself as I dialed the couple of numbers I knew—the widow next door and the man Grandpa had known for longer than I had been alive. I hung up after the second one and just stood there. Neither had seen or heard from him.

I glanced over my shoulder. Seth was elbow deep in something with meringue on it. I thrummed my fingers. Grandpa's favorite place to visit was the library. It was a long shot, but I was desperate.

"The elderly Mr. Turner?" a young female librarian responded to my question about him. "Such a sweet fellow. We just adore him here."

"Have you seen him recently?" I was tempted to hammer the handset on the nearby wall to hurry information out of her.

"He's our best customer. Why, if libraries survived by charging a fee for each book a patron read, he alone could support our whole staff. He checks out at least…"

"Ma'am," I interrupted her. Perspiration beaded my skin. My head pounded with pain. "I just want to know if you have seen him lately."

She harrumphed. "Well, as I was starting to tell you before you interrupted," she paused for effect. Or punishment. "He recently checked out more books than he could carry. In fact, I myself helped him with them."

Grandpa loved to read, but that many books didn't sound right.

"Did he say where he was going?"

"No, I helped him get settled into a taxi, and he was on his way. I did notice how pale he was. Not as steady as usual, either." She paused again. "Do you suppose he was checking into a hospital and that is why he stocked up on reading material? Oh my."

"Thank you for your help, ma'am." I hung up before she could say more. Heroes operated with a plan. My grandfather, my one true hero, evidently had a plan. But what? Looking over my shoulder, I saw Seth finishing off a brownie. No wonder he carried a little extra weight.

I returned to the table and slid into my seat. "Grandpa was last seen at the library checking out a large stack of books."

Seth swiped a well-used napkin across his face and dropped it beside one of his several plates. "So, wherever he went, you think it was for an extended stay. That's good. He's sharp. He is laying low. Unless he's in the hospital."

Residual fury at the librarian rose up. But I choked it back down. "He isn't at a hospital," I snapped. "But I suppose I could call the one he would go to if he did. But he didn't."

"How about I call for you while you order

something to eat. You're looking whitish."

I felt whitish, so I agreed and ordered another tuna fish sandwich along with coffee. By the time my food came, and I choked it down, Seth returned to the table, a little whitish himself.

"I found him." He perched at the edge of his seat.

"Where?"

"At the hospital. Some cab driver drove him there. Said your grandfather didn't look well."

I yanked to my feet. "We need to go back to New York right now."

"Sit down." Seth tried to wave me back to my seat, but I didn't move. "People are staring, and neither of us can afford to be recognized."

I sat. "I'm still going back to New York."

"Not yet. I spoke to your grandfather. He said he's fine, just a little bit of lightheadedness caused the cab driver to worry."

"He's lying."

Seth gave a half shrug. "Could be, but he gave me a phone number for where he is going. The place he intended to go before he was taken to the hospital. A little resort-type place outside the city. He said he was going there so you wouldn't worry about him and could finish your mountain climbing." Seth frowned. "Do you think he's getting senile? This area is as flat as a table."

"No. He's fine. I will explain the mountain climbing some other time. The important thing is, he took my warning seriously and is going to hide somewhere." I thrummed the table in a combination of relief and worry. Any number of people there would check on him for me, but would that endanger him? I thrummed harder. "I can't stand it. I'm going back there and keep an eye on him."

"He said to remind you of something he told you when you were a little boy." Seth said it before I was halfway to my feet. "It doesn't make a lot of sense to me, but most of what your grandfather says baffles me."

I returned to my seat.

"He said, 'No hero ever mistakenly dies at the hand of another. All heroes die exactly where they are supposed to and at the exact right time, because that is the place and time they chose.' "

Seth and I sat without saying a word while the waitress lugged away a large collection of dishes and dinnerware, leaving a hefty tab behind. I gladly swiped it off the table. I owed Seth a lot.

"We're staying, aren't we?" Seth asked.

Did heroes cry? I wanted to. Should I stay here and finish Grandpa's and my story like he wanted me to? Because we were both heroes choosing where we would be? And might die? Even if the one we loved brought our death about? Sure not. Surely Chastity wouldn't…wasn't… Surely her questions about my grandfather were nothing but sincere.

"Let's stay long enough to turn in my article about Hitler's deserter to the newspaper in Chicago. That might be the best way to get whoever killed Reed off our trail." And Grandpa's.

I paid the tab while Seth got the address to what some believed to be the second largest newspaper in the US. *Someday I will wake up from this*, I told myself as we drove away from the café. *The greatest story I've ever known, the greatest passion I've ever felt, and the most danger I've ever faced, will all have been a dream.*

I laid a hand on the pouch beneath my shirt. Which meant my story and Chastity's never truly existed.

Chapter 24

Getting out of what some called the *Trib* became tricky. One of the employees recognized me as soon as Seth and I entered the newspaper's building, their excitement causing fans to flock my way, all of them starry-eyed and requesting autographs. I should have worn a disguise, but I had become so immersed in being Jim, the wedding planner deeply in love with the bride, I had forgotten how to be Jim Turner the crime writer.

While Seth reveled in the attention, I kept asking for the editor who handled news articles about the war as I scribbled my name on any scrap of paper shoved my way. When at last someone listened to my request and led us to the right office, my fans followed, more joining them as we went.

As if that wasn't bad enough, the editor recognized me for my articles written for the *Times* and about swallowed himself when I offered him Reed's. He frowned as he read it, then looked up when he finished.

"This isn't your usual stuff," he said to me.

By the time Seth explained Reed's death and the uncertainty he and I faced, Chicago's largest newspaper not only took my article but offered me any penthouse I wanted in their city if I would stay and write for them. Maybe Ruth and Grandpa were right and I was meant to write stories from and of the heart. I shuddered. What heart? Mine was shattered. All I wanted to do was give them the story and hope the right thugs saw it. Then leave.

"I knew you were popular, Jim, but I had no idea you were *that* popular," Seth said when we finally left the waving, admiring throng at the newspaper.

"Do you think this will work?" I asked, cutting into his laud and amazement. "Do you think this paper can get that article out where we want it?" I was thinking of Grandpa, not of myself. If this rendition of the deserter spared anyone, I wanted it to be my grandfather.

"You have to realize that the *Times* will pick it up once it goes AP, so, yes, whoever killed Reed and is looking for you will see it."

"Will it make a difference?" My head was splitting. I could barely think. All I knew was that Grandpa had to be safe.

Seth tipped his head as if pondering his answer as he maneuvered his car through Chicago's streets, which were busy, but not nearly as busy as New York's. "If that was me you wrote about, my wife would be in heaven with pleasure. I don't know how you, a good-guy-versus-bad-guy sort of writer, came up with that much heart, but it's good. Even I saw Hitler's ex-soldier as a man above all men. You made me forget his heinous side as I took in someone I will idolize forever."

I believed Seth, for once. My editor, who had lied to keep me working for him for years, was finally telling the truth. I relaxed a bit. All of us, especially Grandpa, might be safer once the article hit the streets.

"Pull over," I said as I pointed at a phone booth on a street corner.

"That's pretty risky," Seth replied as he found a spot to park. "It's not dark out yet, and that booth is pretty obvious."

"Just keep an eye out. I want to talk to my grandfather." Carrying the piece of paper where Seth had written Grandpa's destination, I scurried from the car and hurried to the booth. I called the hospital first, assuming he would actually still be there.

"I'm sorry, sir. Mr. Turner checked out about an hour ago," a hospital nurse explained.

"Did he leave with a bunch of books?" I asked while my mind raced with all sorts of reasons why Grandpa should have stayed where they could keep an eye on his health.

"A whole bunch." She laughed. "I hope someone is at his house to help him inside with them."

I thanked her. Grandpa wasn't going home, but I called his number there anyway. No one answered, so I tried the resort he told Seth he would stay at. They hadn't seen him either. Though it was summer, and Chicago radiated with heat, I felt chilled. "Be all right, Grandpa." I hung up the phone, checked the crowds swarming past and around the phone booth, then darted to Seth's car. I would call the resort again when we reached my hotel. "Be all right, Grandpa," I whispered again.

Chapter 25

To my relief, I was told Grandpa had checked into his room at the resort when I called from my hotel's lobby phone. They gave me a private number to reach him.

"You are there," I gasped. *And alive.* I felt giddy.

Grandpa chuckled at my greeting, music to my ears. "I took the scenic route, I guess. Sure didn't mean to. Overly cautious cab driver." He chuckled again.

I didn't tell him the librarian thought he looked gaunt when she saw him. He was either lying to protect me or truly felt good for his age and condition, neither of which I would ruin with a rebuttal. "I'm glad you are safe. And well," I added, though I wasn't convinced.

"I will be fine here, son. Quite honestly, I would have been fine at home as well, but if my being here gives you peace of mind enough to stay and finish what you have to do there, then I am happy to do it."

"Thank you. I do feel better there are other eyes and ears around you. I can't believe you have a phone in your room, by the way. That is wonderful."

"Top-notch place, considering the war is drawing our resources. I will tip them heavily when I leave."

"I will be right there with you when you do," I promised and tried to envision it: life like it used to be, his in particular.

"To the best of my ability, I will wait for you." The

silence following was neither of us adding to what we worried might not happen.

"Here is what I know as of now." I charged past our shaky quiet. "Seth is with me, both of us watching our backs. We turned in my rendition of the deserter's story to a Chicago newspaper, hoping to pacify whoever tried to stop Reed's version, who we assume is the deserter. Honestly, that's the only reason we're still here. If someone is after us, we won't bring them close to you or Seth's wife. We're coming back to New York as soon as we're pretty sure it is safe."

"There is more."

I sighed. "Not really."

"You're a good storyteller, Jim, but a poor liar."

The wind went out of me. Like an empty sack, I wanted to crumple to the floor. "Not really anything essential," I tried. When Grandpa didn't respond, I dragged a nearby chair close with the toe of my shoe and sat. Heavily. "I was duped. Which stalls the story I was writing with your gold pen. The deserter's part is the only one I understand. He lived as a true self-sacrificing hero who was willing to die to protect the one he loves. As for your part of the story, I really don't know what happened, Grandpa. I only have pieces of it. And as for my part...if I hadn't written it in ink, I would erase every single word because none of it turned out to be true."

I slumped in the chair and tipped my aching head back.

"This is a conversation I would prefer to have face to face, son, but that's not possible, so listen carefully to everything I have to say."

I straightened. "I will."

"You haven't heard the end of the deserter's story

yet, you know that. And you are missing some of the earlier parts, as well."

"Grandpa, we both know I can only get that from him or his lover. If he gets that close to me…"

"Then you will listen to him as carefully as you should to me." Thankfully he didn't add an "if you get the chance," though we both knew that was true. Instead, Grandpa cleared his throat. "As for my story, I have been giving it to you in bits and pieces over the years. You couldn't have taken it in all at once. Nor would you have understood."

Not like I would now. Grove, Grandpa's peninsula, Mountain Grove…and Chastity…had all given me ears to hear. Those poetic pearls of wisdom he had shared with me since childhood gathered in my thoughts, not yet a cohesive story. His hints of love and heroes' hearts I had scoffed at joined my memories.

"Let me tell it," I said, sitting even straighter in my chair. "You fill in the blanks."

"I will, son."

"You came to Grove, Illinois…"

"By accident, it would have seemed. An unscheduled stop by a train that turned out to be serendipitous."

"Because you got off the train…"

"When she did."

I gasped. "She was on the train with you?" My thoughts reeled. Grandpa hadn't met her in Grove, he came to know her better in Grove.

"We were both on our way to visit partners we had been seeing for some time. She to a young man in Chicago, and me to…well, you know who I eventually married. Anyway, the woman I met on the train had been working as a schoolteacher in Nebraska, and I was on my way home after a stint with the service."

"By the time the train reached Grove, and stopped, she had your heart."

"And I couldn't let her unknowingly take it with her once the train resumed its course. Not that I wanted it back. In fact, I never did get it back. What I had hoped was for all of me—heart, soul, mind, and body—to be with her forever. It almost happened that way. But my body was all I had with me when we left Grove."

Parts of Grandpa had remained in Grove. I had felt him so strongly when I was there. I had even seen him when I looked at myself in the mirror. He was on the peninsula as well, he and... "Yellow. She had blonde hair?"

"Yellow was her favorite color. I called her the center of my daisy when I plucked its petals saying, 'She loves me, she loves me not.' Because how we felt anchored in her. She was the vibrant yellow center, the sun everything revolved around. At least for me."

My skin turned cold. Had what happened to me also happened to him? An unfaithful woman using him somehow? "I'm sorry, Grandpa..."

"No need to be, son. She felt strongly about me."

"Then why? That is the part I don't know. Why didn't you stay with her, and marry her?"

"The answer to that is on the peninsula. I wanted you to find it."

"Find what? Where exactly?"

"I buried all that was left of our short time together right beneath where the two of us stood near the tip. Find it before you come back, son. It's time."

I wanted to argue, but I didn't. Grandpa had never

been forthright in anything he divulged. He felt learning was best done by living with obscure signs along the way that made a person think. "I will go find it," I promised, though he and I both knew whatever he buried could be long gone. And I could get arrested for destruction of public property. Seth would have a fit.

"The wedding is tomorrow," Grandpa said, catching me off guard.

I made a bluster of noises, none of them real words. So unlike a true writer. "Not that it matters," I finally spewed. Then I described Chastity's life of lies, her escape, her other persona hidden below her house. "Whether there is a Dwayne or not, I doubt she ever spoke a word of truth to me." Or to her parents, since she apparently duped them into decorating the peninsula. With that thought, I didn't need my evil side to suggest I dig holes in the ground during Chastity's wedding. It would serve her right if I unearthed something which spoke of real love while she lived her sham.

"Remember what I said about heroes choosing where they stand or fall?" Grandpa asked instead of rallying behind my fury. "Choose and choose wisely. Act, don't react. You will get caught in an avalanche and never make it to the mountain's top if you don't make that distinction."

My anger waned enough for me to see it was nothing more than a heart so broken it was fighting for any life at all. I slumped again. "Were you furious when you left Grove?"

"No." He coughed then, a wheezy hack followed by a yawn. I had taxed the man I loved more than I loved myself, and I had done it right after he left the hospital.

"I'm sorry, Grandpa. Go rest. Get a good night's

sleep. I will call you tomorrow. And I love you."

"I love you too. Now go finish our stories, especially yours. You have a lot of writing to do."

I hung up and stared at the quiet telephone. Such irony. The deserter had a story, Grandpa had a story, even the short brown-haired woman who led me to Chastity had a story. At least she said she did. Grandpa said I had one, as well. I laid a hand on all of them, feeling another story in the pouch with ours. Chastity's. Not a story I wanted to read, but I had to. Because when I took my stand as a hero, a stand where I would either live or die, I wanted to choose that spot wisely.

Chapter 26

Seth joined me, and I welcomed him, as we holed up in my hotel room with food and iced teas…and Chastity's book. Seth brought a chair close to the dresser top where we spread the food next to my typewriters, and I sat propped up in the bed, pillows behind my aching head, my plate on the bedside table.

"Here goes," I said and extracted her book from my hidden pouch. I wouldn't be able to eat a bite. Just like my lunch, I was certain Seth would eventually devour mine.

A lemony scent wafted up from the cover and pages, a powerful jolt to a heart which lay in pieces. Blonde curls, blue eyes, and the face that had swept me off my feet in an instant, swirled in a cloud of memories around me. "Chastity." I pressed my palm against the book's cover, letting an essence I had failed to resist touch me once again. Touch and no more, though. Because I shuddered at what I might find within it.

Truth or lies? I wondered as I peered within at an indiscriminate page. She had left this journal behind. On purpose? As a part of her ruse? Or by mistake? Was the real Chastity…or Margie…in here?

"What's it say?" Seth queried between bites of his sandwich. If he had been Grandpa, I would ask him to read it aloud for me. But Seth…even though he had improved…hadn't come far enough to be trusted with such a moment as this.

"Random page," I said. Forcing myself to focus and read her words, I was shocked to find mine instead.

"A vacuum will surround Shale Lake's peninsula on June 20th. On that afternoon, as happened at Creation, love will take pieces of Chastity and Dwayne and unite them in an explosion of life. Anyone nearby will be transformed by the fallout, the twinkling sensation of stars, sunlight, and water, as they commit their love forever."

June twentieth was tomorrow. Maybe there really was a Dwayne. "I wrote that the first day I met her," I explained to Seth, whose brows bunched into a frown. "Don't worry. She had quite an effect on me. I became unrecognizable." I became like my grandfather.

"What did she have to say? Did she write something after that?"

I didn't want to look, but I did. "Written for me and about me by Jim Turner, my answer to prayer." That was the truth as far as she had said it to me. Seth raised a brow but shrugged and dug into another sandwich. I chose a couple of other random pages to read and found more notes regarding things she had said that I already knew. Which made Chastity seem ordinary and innocent, not conniving and sinister.

"Skip the middle," Seth suggested. "You know the middle of any book lacks tension. It's the beginning and the ending that matter." My astute editor was right.

With trembling hands, I went to the front of the book and found it to be the beginning of her relationship with Dwayne, who really did exist. I cleared my throat and began to read aloud. "He said he was looking for someone when I met him. Though I wasn't that person, he said I was better. And that maybe he was meant to meet me all along."

"Who?" Seth barked. "Who was he really supposed to find?"

"She doesn't say." I scoured the page and the ones following, seeing the thread of a developing relationship with nothing concrete about Dwayne other than how he looked, how he treated her, and how much she missed him when he was gone. But he always returned. Just like she insisted he would again tomorrow to marry her.

"I don't trust him, whoever he is," Seth stated.

"I never did." Though I had reasons more personal than Seth's. That familiar defensiveness rose up inside of me, the one which fell in love with Chastity and despised her fiancé. I set her journal aside. "I don't think I can read this."

Seth rose to his feet and dusted crumbs to the floor. "I can." For a pudgy, out-of-shape man, he moved pretty quickly. He had Chastity's book in his hands before I could stop him. He flipped to the last page and frowned at whatever she had written there, then looked up. "She says here, 'He will come. I know he will. Even if things aren't quite the way I planned.' "

A pang of guilt pierced me. No matter what else this girl was involved in, she still wanted a wedding. That I had failed to help her with. "I will take the cot." I rose to my feet. No matter how long I had known Seth, I couldn't fathom fitting onto a bed comfortably with him. "Take the bed. You can have my sandwich, too. I don't want to hear anymore from Chastity's book. See you in the morning."

Chapter 27

Before the sun came up…or Seth rose…I knew what I had to do. Bathing and changing quietly, I left him asleep, Chastity's book beside him, my half-eaten sandwich on the bedside table next to him. Quietly locking the door behind me, I walked through the early morning light to the hotel lobby, looked around outside its door, and then stepped inside.

"Good morning, sir."

I jumped at the familiar greeting, then relaxed when I spotted a desk clerk I had never seen before.

"Can I help you with something?" he queried.

"Newspaper?"

"Yes, sir. Right here. We provide both of Chicago's papers." He pointed to two stacks so fresh I could smell the ink from across the lobby. "Help yourself."

I did, thanking him. Stepping outside and well beyond his range of sight, I looked through the *Trib* for what I knew would be there. Sure enough, they hadn't wasted any time.

"He Did It for Love," the title read, the subtitle, "Man Sacrifices All to Save One."

I knew what the article said, but I read it anyway, praying the deserter was seeing it at the same time. Grandpa also. The *Trib*, in their desperation to woo me as a writer, had kept my name off it, just as I had asked. Reed wasn't mentioned anywhere either. I rolled the paper up when finished and smacked it against my open palm while I gazed around at a half-full parking lot. No movement anywhere, no beady eyes watching me.

I returned to my room, roused Seth, and headed to Grandpa's peninsula for the rest of my plan. If I lived through it without trouble, I would take that as a sign I could go home to my grandfather. And to re-figure out who Jim Turner was.

Seth pulled up to Shale Lake and parked, its water barely a glimmer through the shallow stretch of trees. We sat and stared at the early morning serenity for several minutes, not another person in sight at this hour. For which I was thankful, since I had a shovel with me, borrowed from the hotel's gardener.

"Do you want to know what else I read in Chastity's book last night?" Seth broke the silence.

Yes. "No."

"You're a terrible liar."

"So I've been told. But I fooled her, and that is good enough."

Seth snorted. "That's what you think. She knew more about you than you did."

My face probably reddened. It felt warm. Thankfully it wasn't fully light yet, and Seth wasn't all that perceptive. "That was part of the problem. She knew who I was, but I had no idea about her."

"And based on this sub-par information, you still want to make sure her wedding is set up the way she wanted it before we dig?"

"I promised." It was the least I could do, and the most I ever would since she would have Dwayne from now on. That hurt terribly. But, in time, I would experience relief. Probably. Maybe. "Let's get this done before anyone shows up."

Seth and I climbed out of the car, retrieved the shovel, and strode to Grandpa's peninsula. We stopped beneath the shelter, this strange and blissful place oddly eerie in the light of dawn. The waves were quieter than they were when the sun was fully up, the wind softer, Chastity's wedding fixtures silently waiting.

"Are you sure about this?" Seth asked again. I nodded. "Then here is your list."

"What?"

"Right here on this post." Seth walked to the shelter's corner and took down a note someone had tacked up. Sure enough it was the final To-Do list for Chastity's wedding. "It's like she knew you were coming." He paused. "Do you think we're safe here…" He cast a wary glance around. "Just because the article is out doesn't mean anyone has seen it yet. Not the ones we hope will see it, anyway."

"The list could just be a reminder to herself. Or to her parents." But if Seth was right, and she expected me to show up here, I either really was her answer to prayer or a stoolie with a target on my back. "Is my name on it anywhere?"

We both checked her list. It was her handwriting but addressed to no one in particular. The only good thing I could think, regarding this, was that if she had set me up because of Reed, then Grandpa would be safe. I took the note from Seth's hand.

"Thread greenery and flowers through arch. Put remainder in vases at the arch's sides. Set up serving table under shelter and overlay it with a tablecloth, pinning it at the corners. Make sure the chairs are straight."

"Thread greenery?" Seth sputtered. "If we're going to be shot, I sure don't want my final picture to be of me with flowers and vines in my hands."

He made a good point. Grandpa might understand a final tribute of that sort, but my fans never would. "I'm taller, so the archway will be easier for me. I will take care of the threading while you do the tablecloth and straighten the chairs."

"Only for you," Seth grumbled, and we set to work, everything we needed to complete Chastity's list already there and waiting.

The trellis-type arch proved to be a challenge, and poking plants through the holes seemed much more expedient than threading. Dwayne was tall, taller than me, apparently. He had to duck anyway, so he could duck a little more to avoid the dangling, low-hanging stems.

By the time we finished, daylight fell upon Grandpa's peninsula and Shale Lake. Though we should hurry, the draw to stand at the tip near the shore beckoned Seth and me both. Pink light danced on waves that had now awakened, the breeze catching the scent of fresh water and damp earth.

"What's the word I want?" Seth asked from my side. "And please don't say 'beautiful.'"

"Criminally beautiful."

Seth laughed, but I hurt. Chastity and I had shared our own laughter over that very remark. Sadness returned and weighed me down. Was this how Grandpa felt the last time he stood here?

I walked back to the shelter where we had left the shovel, Seth alongside me.

"Even though this didn't turn out to be a setup, we

should probably still hurry," he commented, looking at the morning light.

Chastity's wedding, which apparently was real and not part of her deception, was to be later in the day, but he was right. Heroes chose places and made plans. If I saw Chastity again, it wouldn't be by accident. I wanted to be ready.

Grabbing the shovel, I stood at the shelter's edge and looked toward the water. Somewhere between this spot and the peninsula's tip, Grandpa had buried my answer. I paced toward the shore and stopped well before it, not far from where Chastity would wed later. Maybe Dwayne would trip and fall if I left the dirt soft. With that thought, I chose a spot and dug in. Gently. Whatever Grandpa left here could be near the surface, and it would be old. I wanted his treasure in its entirety, not broken.

By the time my shovel's tip clinked against something solid, the sun had risen enough to bring early fishermen and boaters to Shale Lake.

"Is that it?" Seth raced to my side, abandoning his prior pacing, which he had referred to as guard duty. He bent close as I dropped to my knees and worked at the dirt with my fingers.

"I believe so," I huffed as I cleared dirt from a rectangular metal box, a small tin that had held up well as I lifted it from its hole. My heart hammered. My grandfather's soul was in this, the pieces of him he had tried to share with me my whole life. The part he left behind but chose me to retrieve for him. And write about. The old Seth would have tossed this into the lake to preserve the Jim Turner whose stories made most of his living for him. But this Seth…

"There is something sacred about this," he said in

awe. Then he blushed.

I rose to my feet, kicking loose dirt back into the hole, looking around between kicks. "How about we open it in the shelter?" On a table out of sight of passersby.

Seth joined me, snatching up the shovel I had laid aside. Together we chose a table which gave us some anonymity near a cluster of trees, then dropped onto bench seats opposite each other. I wished Grandpa were here doing the honors to his past. The sense of him returned in full, his tall, younger version standing at the peninsula's point with...

Securely clasped, but not locked, the lid opened surprisingly easily. Seth and I nearly banged heads, each of us so eager to see what my grandfather had hidden inside. A cloth, for starters. Not oiled but waxy, effective for fending off moisture. I removed it from the box and slowly unfolded it to four things I hadn't imagined—two rings and two train tickets.

While Seth scooted to the edge of his seat, I lifted each gold ring, one larger than the other. "His and hers," I said. Evidently never used. But why not? "Check the tickets," I said to Seth, who had almost passed out with excitement.

His pudgy fingers moved with amazing stealth as he opened the tickets fully and laid them flat in front of us. One had Gerald Turner written on it. Grandpa. The other had a woman's name, Gloria Swenson.

"I have no idea," I said to Seth's querying look regarding her name. "Not my grandmother, though." While I stared at the gold bands now on my fingers, Seth studied the tickets. Finally he let out a low whistle.

"I think I understand." He looked up and situated the

two tickets so I could read them. "They are tickets *to* here. Not from here."

I snatched them closer. Seth was right. Both to Grove, and neither stamped. Never used. Just like these rings. "This only tells me what didn't happen, but I still don't know why." I sounded frustrated, which was wrong. Grandpa said my answer was here, so it would be. "Evidently they planned to marry. Probably here. Maybe after they broke up with their respective partners and then returned to Grove. But it never got that far. The whole wedding was abandoned before they left here, otherwise the tickets wouldn't be in this tin box, only the rings would be, because they would have taken their tickets with them."

I searched the rings for any engraving while Seth pored over the tickets for anything we might have missed. In desperation I picked up the waxy cloth and gave it a good shake. A slender, brown, dried leaf floated to the table's top. We both reached for it, but I pinched it up first and held it where we could both study it.

"Not important." Seth dismissed it. "Just some weed that got in the box by mistake."

"It's no mistake," I corrected him, twisting it in my fingertips. "Nor is it a weed. Or a leaf. This is an old daisy petal." I laid it on the wax cloth. One petal. "She loves me," I said.

"She loves me not," Seth corrected me. "I bet it's the last petal."

"No, it's the first. If he meant 'She loves me not,' he would have included two."

Just as we had before I came to Grove, Seth and I fell into a disagreement, each of us wielding either "She loves me" or "She loves me not" at the other. Our voices rose along with our adamancy that the other was wrong—until I heard my name stated in a deep tone.

"Turner."

Seth and I both quieted and gazed at the tall figure at the back entrance to the shelter. He stayed to the shadows, his gaze fixed on me.

"You have certainly complicated things," he said in the same deep tone.

I detected no accent, so I wasn't looking at Hitler's deserter. Neither did he fit the description Reed had given me. But... I rose to my full height, stretched painfully even a bit higher, and still my eyes didn't reach the level of his.

"You did come," I said when I realized who he was.

"Of course. I said I would." Did Dwayne smirk? The shadows on his face that was practically in the rafters hid his expression.

My mind raced for something to say that didn't give away the fear which suddenly crawled up my spine. "Then you will be happy to know everything is ready for your wedding." I swiped my arm through the air, indicating all that had been set up ahead of time.

"Like I said, you have certainly complicated things." It wasn't a possible smirk this time, it was anger. Sourness. Peevish irritation as if I was a fly in his ointment.

"Complicated things? I will have you know I played a big part in preparing for your ceremony."

Dwayne stepped into the light then, his face coming out from the shadows. He did resemble me. Physically. Sort of. But I lacked his piercing stare. "You write books. You know what it is to create a false front."

"False front? Your wedding is a false front?" My

voice grew louder and higher. I truly had been fooled. Not just by Chastity, but also by…

No. The steely smirk on Dwayne's face told me I wasn't the only victim. His fiancée had been fooled as well. "Is that all Chastity meant to you? I can't believe anyone would do such a thing to her." My fists bunched. I planted them on the table, no longer competing to look taller than Dwayne. Fiercer meant more now. How dare this creep treat Chastity that way!

Dwayne laughed. Not a pretty laugh, either. One which made Seth gasp as he watched the fiend with rounded eyes. "Don't get your Maid of Honor hackles up. I needed the wedding, and she needed a husband. Did she tell you her reason? Do you know why getting married was so important to her?"

My gut roiled. Never had I written a character so foul as Dwayne. I was right to despise him from the very beginning. "You misunderstood her," I seethed. "She was thrilled to be marrying you. She defended you. She… She…" She wanted what I wrote in her invitation and her announcement. Hadn't she said herself that I had written what she felt to her very depths?

"I know. She wanted love. But she also needed a marriage." Dwayne shrugged. "Don't delude yourself that you understand her or would be better for her than I will be. You two have known each other for what? Three days? Did she ever once say she loved you? Wanted you? I doubt it."

She hadn't said she loved me, nor had I said it to her. My mind whirled with what was true about her and what was not. She inferred a lifelong commitment to me, but she never veered from her promise to Dwayne. I glared at the tall man poised not far away. "Why did you want

227

a wedding?"

Dwayne looked at me for a long moment. "Because of Reed."

Now I gasped along with Seth.

"Like I said, you really complicated things. Reed came out of nowhere and unwittingly gathered more information than the imbecile knew in his glory-seeking nosiness. It was just a matter of time before he put two and two together then blabbed things no one was to know. He wasn't liked, but pretty well known, so my job was to fit in, look like an ordinary guy while I waited for just the right moment to stop him. I admit, we didn't see you coming. We had been able to thwart any glory-seeking journalist from doing that interview he foolishly offered. We never suspected a crime novelist who wrote soft war stories part time, would take it on."

If we weren't so terrified, Seth probably would have glared at me and I at him over whose fault it was I did the article. Unfortunately, Seth would be right to blame me.

"Who is 'we'?" I asked.

One side of Dwayne's mouth kicked up in a crooked grin. "You probably think 'we' is Hitler's deserter and me. Think again. Reed's buffoonery got the deserter's attention, but you caused him to slip up. The story you had printed in the newspaper…not so bright a move as you probably thought. No man with the deserter's background or in his position can risk a single pitter-patter of the heart. That split second of distraction was enough to get him killed. So Herr Hitler and I thank you."

I dropped to the table's bench. I had cost the deserter his life while trying to save my own? And Grandpa's?

The air felt heavy, my body like lead. I had destroyed the very hero I had come to admire. And envy. Reed's story didn't leave the deserter's lover vulnerable, I had.

I stared dumbly at the two gold rings still on my fingers. My grandfather was a hero who chose. He chose, for whatever reason, to leave these and their train tickets behind. He chose to forego marrying Gloria Swenson, whoever she was. While I stupidly sat and learned all of Dwayne's secrets. I was losing my life, not choosing to give it up. Dwayne would never let Seth or me live to tell what we now knew, any more than Reed had been allowed to. The only thing I didn't know was why. Why my grandfather left the one he loved so deeply.

Maybe Dwayne enjoyed my misery he didn't understand, for he watched as I peeled the two wedding bands off my fingers and set them on the table. He probably enjoyed a wrong assumption that I was morose about dying, as I slid the waxed cloth in front of me and laid the rings on it. I picked up the two tickets to refold when something thin flittered out of one and landed on the table. Seth and I both stared at it, then at each other. He was right. The second dried daisy petal.

"She loves me not," we said together.

"I told you that," Dwayne sneered.

We ignored him. Now I knew what I came here to find. Grandpa had let go of his heart and the very blood that pulsed through it because he detected something less in hers. He didn't overrun Gloria, tell himself he could make her happy, that she would learn to love him in the same way he loved her, with time, or that she could be satisfied with his pure devotion. He didn't make Gloria a prisoner to his own passion. He set her free so she could hopefully find what he had found in her. His was love at its perfection.

Which was what Chastity should have. It was certainly what she wanted. And it was not what Dwayne offered her.

"Are you girls about finished?" Dwayne scoffed.

"Almost." I refolded everything of Grandpa's into the waxed cloth and enclosed it inside the tin container. Metaphorically, I was wrapping my heart, my desire to marry Chastity, my means of marrying her, and hiding it along with Grandpa's inside the tin. Each of the heroes in my story died some sort of death, the deserter's a physical death from the sound of it. Grandpa's a death to the bond he still wanted. And mine... I looked up at Dwayne's leer as he watched me. That face represented the disregard that would kill me and then cheat Chastity out of any chance for real love. The sort of love I would set her free to have. Now.

I leapt from the table. For an out-of-shape writer, I shocked myself. And Dwayne. I thrust myself into his chest, striking something hard, which was likely a gun beneath his jacket. We hit the ground, him on his back and me on top of him. I grappled for the gun, unsuccessfully. Dwayne was like a spider, eight arms and legs, all quick and strong. Suddenly there were two more arms in the tangle Dwayne and I found ourselves in. To my surprise, they were Seth's. The saying that writers limit themselves to what they know proved true as Seth's and my knowledge of how to fight slowly succumbed to Dwayne's expertise. What I knew as the crime writer, and Seth knew by editing my work, paled in comparison to what Dwayne knew from experience.

I saw a flash of metal as Dwayne sent me sprawling to one side. Before I regained my balance, he was on his feet with Seth, a pistol pointed at my editor. And friend. My family.

"You're both dead anyway," Dwayne seethed, not nearly as out of breath as Seth and I were. "But you can decide when and where."

Choose. Heroes chose their appointed time and place to die. Grandpa couldn't possibly have meant that in this context, at the mercy of a coldblooded killer who offered options.

Seth's eyes were wide with terror. I wouldn't let him end this way any more than I would let Chastity live her life without love. The kind I had for her, and Grandpa had for Gloria. The kind that died and let go to free another.

"I choose out there," I shouted, my arm like an arrow pointing at Shale Lake. It accomplished what I hoped, a split second of confusion for Dwayne. Like the split second the deserter's heart must have pitter-pattered at my article. I saw the opportunity and I dove.

An ear-splitting shot pierced the air. So did Seth's scream. All three of us hit the ground, Dwayne on the bottom, me on top, and my editor sandwiched in between. I started swinging. How dare this viper of a man shoot my friend! My fury raged, my arms entangled with others, my threats meshed with warnings, until someone yanked me off the ground. Another person did the same with Seth. No one touched Dwayne. He just lay there.

I couldn't breathe deeply enough as I stared at Chastity's fiancé, who no longer resembled me since I was alive and he didn't seem to be. Whoever held me back let go of my arms. A man I had never seen before let go of Seth.

"What happened?" I gazed at the four men standing around us. And at one small, brown-haired, plain-looking woman who stepped forward and walked around Dwayne's still body before she stopped in front of me.

"I had a story," she said. Almost the same way she'd said it years ago. No, that was three days ago. Outside of Chastity's home. "You just finished it. Thank you. I knew you could." She gave me a simple smile and turned to the four men, the movement causing a nearly hidden badge to glint in the sun.

Seth and I buoyed each other up as Dwayne was carried off on a stretcher. I could see the blood now, but the short woman said he wasn't dead. She had questions for us, and I had plenty for her, so she arranged to drive Seth and me to their office. Something they had set up locally and temporarily until Dwayne could be caught. We protested we could drive ourselves, which she politely but firmly refused, saying we were both in shock.

Seth grabbed the shovel and I snatched up Grandpa's tin. She was right. We were in shock as we staggered after her and the men. But not enough shock for me to miss stopping near the chairs we had organized for Chastity's service.

"What about the wedding?" I asked. "Shouldn't the bride be told?"

The small, brown-haired woman paused and looked at me. "She knows." She turned and my stomach sank. Seth and I followed her to the car.

Chapter 28

I never let go of Grandpa's tin containing the daisy petals, his unused wedding rings and train tickets. They were his fantasy that never ended for him, a moment which lasted forever. I kept it in my hand while answering far more questions than either Seth or I had imagined, the two of us having only brushed against the tip of Hitler's iceberg, which stretched deeper into this country than even I, as a writer for the *Times,* would have guessed. Possibly an ex-writer for the *Times.* Neither Seth nor I intended to return any of their calls until this was thoroughly cleared up and in our pasts.

"What about the stout woman who warned me I was being watched?" I asked the short, brown-haired woman whose name turned out to be Dixie, once it was our turn to ask questions.

"She is one of us," Dixie answered, the agent next to her nodding. Though the room they chose carried a stark barrenness that made it seem Seth and I were being interrogated as criminals, she assured us it was one of their better conference areas and to relax. To prove it, she brought us cups of coffee and a plate of cookies.

"How about Wally from the hotel?" I asked after a sip of far-too-strong coffee.

"We haven't picked him up yet, but we know where he is. He's holed up in a small town in Vermont, hiding from us and from those he originally helped, meaning

233

Hitler's supporters. He panicked when he saw Dwayne shoot Reed and crumbled when pressured about it by another group. He will be flown to Chicago shortly."

"So that's who he meant when he said someone tall had killed Reed," I said as Seth and I exchanged a surprised look.

"Exactly. You were right not to trust Wally. Turns out no one could. The other hotel clerk, Kevin, wasn't with them or us. Just a guy doing his job."

"Is my contact with the *Times* all right?" Seth asked. "He seemed to vanish. Did they…" He paused, a cookie in one hand and coffee in the other.

"He is fine. The one who 'pretended' to be him was one of us. Your contact was kept in a safe location until we were finished." Dixie looked at me. "The one pretending to be the contact intentionally tried to frighten you about Seth. He hoped you would panic and get out of Grove before something happened to you. Like Dwayne getting to you." She leaned back in her chair, then filled us in on other people in the area who had already been picked up or who were about to be. "Dwayne has been stubborn about cooperating, which isn't surprising, but others in his 'ring' haven't been as loyal to the cause. That cause being Hitler's. More than that I cannot divulge. But I can tell you Reed's tale about the deserter and the woman he saved could have exposed more than their escape. So neither the deserter nor the Führer wanted it told, but each for their own reasons."

"Speaking of the deserter… I'm not sure if I want to know this or not, but he…and the woman he saved…"

"The ones you wrote the article about," Dixie stated.

I nodded. "Are they… Is he… Dwayne said, or inferred at least, that the man had been killed." I didn't want him to be dead. Though the possibility was a part of his story and something he was willing to risk, I wanted a happy ending for him.

The male agent reached into a satchel and came out with two photographs, one of a man in a soldier's uniform, the other of an attractive but shy-looking woman with long, wavy brown hair. "We are looking for them for reasons we can't divulge. As for Dwayne's claim the deserter was killed, we don't know."

I pulled the two photographs close and tried not to swallow audibly. I didn't recognize the woman, but him…if he dyed his hair black, I had seen him sitting in my first hotel's lobby hiding behind a newspaper. I couldn't be absolutely positive, but the fleeting glance I got of his profile was pretty convincing. If so, then he too knew I was to interview Randy Reed. He never touched me, but had *he* ransacked my room, instead of Wally? I shoved the pictures back to the agent. No matter how close my brush with death by this man's hand had been, I still wanted him to live. Maybe he had wanted me to live, as well. After all, he, Grandpa, and I had a bond.

"It's nice to put a face with the legend," I said with all the nonchalance I could pretend. I downed the rest of my coffee. "So it was just a fluke that I got caught up in this. If I had stayed in New York, life would have gone on as normal. You would have eventually caught these guys without me being in the way."

Dixie gave us a half smile. "Sort of," she said. "Reed wasn't the easiest man to work around. In fact, we knew nothing about him until he began to draw attention to himself by advertising an exclusive interview guaranteed to expose a war criminal in our country. He got everyone's attention then, not to mention in everyone's way, so we began to monitor who responded to his offer, while trying to keep him protected so we could ferret out Hitler's supporters, whom we were really after. In fact, that was our guy who picked you up at your hotel, Jim, and took you to Reed's room. Anyway, Randy Reed had an overinflated sense of superiority and confidence. As you know, he didn't last long once you spoke to him. How could he, since he provoked two opposing enemies—powerful ones, at that.

"Then, as soon as your editor contacted the *Times* that you would do the article, we were watching you. We were watching you, also," Dixie said to Seth, "but clearly they managed to get close enough to scare you into hiding anyway. We were also keeping an eye on your wife and workplace, if you wondered."

"What about my grandfather?" I was quick to interject.

"Not at first." Dixie shook her head. "We missed his significance until you called him a couple of times. After that, we kept close tabs on him. He was the reason you came to Grove to begin with, right?"

I nodded. "His reasons for my visit here had nothing to do with Reed, though. That was all my doing, to placate a pushy editor." I grinned at Seth's glare…and flushed cheeks.

Dixie fidgeted with the pen she had used while recording Seth's and my answers earlier. "I don't know your thoughts on serendipity, but if anything, your grandfather's wishes for you put you in the right place at the right time to accomplish more than one objective."

Grandpa would like that. Though he was a hero who believed in choosing, his outcomes bore the dreamlike quality of being serendipitous. Like the train that first took him to Grove.

"Speaking of unplanned, what about Clyde? Do you know anything about the ex-con Seth unwittingly set up an interview with?" Once again I gave Seth a sly smile.

"He is back in custody, but he had no part in Hitler's supporters or our plans. He was on the fringes, however, accessible to either, but not directly involved. Wrong place, wrong time, too close to the action, but now he's back behind bars." The male agent fielded that question. Not a surprise, since no one Dixie's size should ever get near a mammoth like Clyde.

We were all quiet, as if we had run out of questions and steam. Dixie and the agent began shuffling their papers and gathering cups and pens. I didn't move. I merely watched, my lips bit between my teeth...fiercely.

"You want to ask, don't you?" She looked at me before she stood.

"I have to know." My voice sounded fragile. Now it was my turn to blush.

"Chastity is exactly as she presents herself. She's a bit of an anomaly. A breath of fresh air in her out-of-the-ordinary way."

I would have termed it extraordinary. At least in the beginning. I kept my lips pinched in a bite that began to hurt. Then I let go. "Is she... Was she..."

"One of ours? In love with Dwayne? Expecting?" Dixie smiled. "I think you should ask her those things."

I wasn't sure whether I could...or would...do that, but one thing I positively wanted to do was to call Grandpa. They led me to an office and left me alone with a telephone on a table beside a comfortable chair. I called the resort first and found Grandpa being packed up to return home.

"This young woman helping me says she's an agent." He chuckled. "I assured her we weren't criminals; you merely wrote about them."

He sounded invigorated, but not as healthy as I wanted him to be. "I am sorry I got all of us into this, especially you," I said.

"This, as you call it, is finished, and it ended well. If you put it into book form, the ending is more than satisfying," Grandpa responded. "What about the other, though? Our real story? It doesn't have to have a happy ending, just the right one."

"I'm working on that," I mumbled.

"Good." He paused. "Did you find…"

"I have everything with me, and I will bring it home to you." I looked at the tin I had only let go of long enough for Dixie and her agent to search through and dismiss it as irrelevant to the case. I hadn't offered to explain there was a tie, albeit a distant one, but neither seemed the type to be interested in my story of heroes and the women they loved.

"I will be waiting," Grandpa said.

"Promise?" I didn't like the way he sounded. Maybe he had been this frail all along and the distance made his weakness seem more evident.

"You don't have to hurry."

We hung up. I believed him. He would be there when I arrived because he missed me as much as I missed him. But also because I carried his eternity in this little tin box. I wouldn't dig around to find Grandpa's Gloria, nor would I ask Dixie, who could most certainly figure out who she was and what happened to her. Grandpa wanted me to write his story, not put an end to it. Just like I wouldn't do anything to interfere in the deserter's final page, merely let him and his love live eternally. Mine was the only ending I was responsible for. And like Grandpa had told me, I was called to walk it out. Then to write what I knew.

One of the agents returned Seth and me to our car, dropping us off in the parking lot and then driving away. Before we climbed inside, I glanced across Shale Lake's shore, waters, and peninsula that had been practically empty this morning. People laughed, enjoyed the sun and water, played and ran, but no one stood at the end of Grandpa's peninsula ready to say, "I do."

I studied the arched trellis and the wilting flowers I had haphazardly left dangling as a snare for Dwayne. Everything was just as Seth and I had arranged and left it, even the mounds of dirt where we had dug up the ground.

"An abandoned wedding site is more eerie than a graveyard," Seth murmured. "Vacated nuptials instead of a vacated body."

I gave him a raised-brow look. "How very literary of you."

"I've been hanging out with you too much the past twenty-four hours. You and your grandpa are rubbing off on me."

I told him to get into his car. Then before I joined him, I took one last panoramic look at Shale Lake and whispered a silent goodbye to Grandpa's peninsula. It was time to go home to New York. But I needed to go to Chastity's before we did.

While Seth waited at the hotel, I drove to Chastity's house and parked alongside her dirt yard. It was right there on the sidewalk that I had first encountered the short, brown-haired woman—Dixie—who told me she had a story. For me to live and finish, it turned out, just as I was doing for my real story.

I climbed out of my car and stared at the ugly building, the precarious balcony, and the rickety ladder. Lemony scent filled the air, an aromatic answer to my doubts billowed from her wide-open windows and door. Chastity really did live here.

In three days, I had fallen completely in love with and had my heart utterly destroyed by her. I could have been killed by her ruse. No. In all honesty, I would have died for her. No hero was simply killed.

Inhaling a scent that had changed me forever, I rounded my car and stood on her patch of dirt. Pastel fabric flapped from her windows and inside her doorway above. I swallowed. Cleared my throat twice, then swallowed again. "Chastity," I fairly bleated and considered running back to my car. Before I could move, yellow caught my eye. I looked to her balcony where blonde curls wafted around her face, bringing one of Grandpa's sayings with it.

Yellow is my favorite color, son. Someday it will be yours as well.

"You came," she said, exactly as she had three days ago when I first stood below her balcony.

"You knew I was coming?"

"No. I only hoped you would."

"How about the first time I was here? Did you know I was coming then?"

"No." Her voice was softer, her expression heavy with misery. "I had no idea."

My traitorous feet took a step toward her ladder while my heart and mind battled it out as to whether I should run to the balcony or away from her.

"All I knew then was that you were Jim Turner, the writer. I recognized you from your books. And I believed you were the answer to my prayers." She held a handful of curls back from her face, leaving her blue eyes vividly clear.

"You said my crime-writing background was what made me so perfect for you. Because I understood urgency, and life-and-death situations. That tells me you knew what sort of man Dwayne was."

"That's the beauty of an answered prayer. Sometimes we don't know what we need, we only think we do. It turns out your criminal expertise was exactly what I needed, but I truly didn't know it yet." The blue in her eyes intensified. Tears. She was either truly remorseful or brokenhearted because she had been duped by someone she loved, just as I had been.

She wiped an errant tear away. "I have to ask you, too, Jim. Did you know what sort of man Dwayne was? Were you planted here by anyone?" She looked genuinely terrified, possibly more afraid I had duped her than that Dwayne had.

I took another step forward, this time by my own will. "No. Absolutely not. I mean, Dixie knew. She baited me, but I knew nothing else at all." Except that I loved Chastity. Not just "had loved" but past, current, and future tense *loved*. She and I had both been fooled, used even. Except...

"Why did you run away? The last time I saw you, you just vanished. I found your journal of notes and the odd furniture under your house, both of which made you seem guilty of deceiving me."

"I was deceiving you, Jim." She hung her head. "I was playing a part to fool you. To fool everyone, including myself. Dwayne did everything right to sweep me off my feet and make me feel special. He even seemed smitten with all of this." She waved a hand toward her home, her plethora of colors and scents. "I was swept off my feet. But I wasn't in love. I didn't realize that until you came along. You genuinely enjoyed me and my quirky lifestyle. You fit me like an odd complement. You gave up everything to help me marry someone you didn't even know. With you, I learned what love really was for the first time. I understand now that Dwayne was merely using me to seem like a normal guy, but you... You treated me so differently. I tried to deny how I felt about you, then hide it, but little truths kept coming out of my mouth and in my book that you took. Maybe you saw the last thing I wrote. 'He will come. I know he will. Even if things aren't quite the way I planned.' That was about you. By the time I was ready to stop trying to fool myself and confess to you how I felt, I learned something about Dwayne. Something horrible that terrified me...for you. I didn't run away from you, I tried to find him. Twice." The cutest face I had ever seen scrunched in pain. "Dixie found me instead. The wedding setup on the peninsula was her idea. I was terrified and angry. I wanted nothing to do with Dwayne..."

"But you did your part to save me and flush him out." I was at the base of her ladder by then. Looking straight up at the girl I had fallen in love with so quickly and so completely...and who I now finally knew had fallen in love with me as well.

Someday, son, something will send your moral compass into a tailspin. Gravity will vanish, and you will fling your guards aside. What has always been singular vision will suddenly become kaleidoscopic. When that happens, grab this pen and write. With blood as your ink, write your heart on the page.

She was up high and I was the one down low, but I felt dizzy enough to topple over. "You know I felt the same as you did, don't you?"

"I knew when I read your story. I saw myself through your eyes, which showed me you and how you felt. Did you ever finish it?"

"I'm finishing it now. Right this very minute."

The best stories are the true ones. They are fantasies when lived.

I grabbed hold of the ladder. "Remember the first time I tried to climb this? I said I couldn't. Just like I said I couldn't help you plan your wedding. But you said we would help each other. 'You be my hero and I will be yours,' you said."

Heroes aren't heroes because they are clever or brave, but because they love someone or something deeply.

I scaled Chastity's ladder like a squirrel. Not only that, I also bounded over her railing like a champion and landed on my feet. With my arms around her, I drew her close. "And Dwayne's baby will be our little secret until it's mine. That is what we will tell everyone."

Her eyes teared again, but she swiped them away. "There is no baby. Apparently I was wrong. Or it wasn't meant to be." More tears pooled in her eyes. "But in any case, clearly I did something with Dwayne I shouldn't have."

"Dwayne's a cad. That part of him bears no resemblance to me." With that, I did what I had wanted to do ever since I laid eyes on Chastity. I met her lips with mine and melded them together forever.

Look for the relationship when you write, son. There always is one, whether it is between a man and a woman, a boy and his dog, a sailor and his ship, or a country and its enemy. The most daring conquests involve the heart. There is no battle, no story, until there is heart.

A word about the author...

Colleen L Donnelly put her science education to use for years, and then put it behind her to pursue other passions. Her first love is writing and her second is hunting - hunting for that next good story, hunting for shed antlers or mushrooms in the woods, hunting for the next good author to read. An avid believer in work hard/play hard, Colleen splits her time between indoors and out, always busy at something.

http://www.colleenldonnelly.com/